About the Author

Matt Wingett is a writer and public speaker with a love of Portsmouth local history, the strange and the unexplained. A former scriptwriter on ITV's police show *The Bill*, he has written short stories, local history and articles for the national press.

He is the author of *Conan Doyle and the Mysterious World of Light, 1887-1920*, *Portsmouth A Literary and Pictorial Tour* and *The Snow Witch*. He republishes classic local history books, and has produced an acclaimed facsimile of the scarce first edition of Conan Doyle's *A Study In Scarlet*. His collaborations with other writers include *Day of the Dead, Portsmouth Fairy Tales for Grown-Ups, Dark City* and *Pompey Writes*.

He lives in Southsea, and loves Pompey, the town of his birth.

A Life Is Amazing Paperback

Mysteries of Portsmouth

First published 2019 by Life Is Amazing
ISBN: 978-1-913001-03-2
First Edition

CONTENTS

INTRODUCTION

MYSTERIOUS CITY

Ghosts, UFOs, Arthurian legends, lost lands, curses, witches and magic... How exactly are mysteries born?

If you ask Sherlock Holmes, Conan Doyle's great detective who was invented in Portsmouth in 1886, he will probably drily point out that not having an answer is the starting point.

But he might also observe that mysteries make some people uneasy, and for them, *any* answer will do. That is surely how some myths and legends are born. Whether they begin by trying to answer who is buried in a Neolithic grave, or asking what a mysterious light in the sky might be, for some, a *wrong* answer is better than *none*.

Sometimes, mistaken identity turns out to be the seed of a mystery, or a myth is sparked from a whispered rumour, catches light and spreads like wildfire.

Some people make up myths on purpose to distract you from something else that's happening.

A friend might want to brighten up your life with a story he swears is true, or maybe he wants to feel like the one who knows the big secret.

Honest mistakes make mysteries, too. A journalist trying to make sense of unclear information might inadvertently create a myth; or he might add two and two and suddenly make five.

Sometimes, the need for an interesting story invites a few juicy embellishments...

From there, it's only a short step to creating a whole new story from nothing - and behold, an urban legend is born - be that for fun, for entertainment, or to make a point. There are so many ways to make mysteries!

Over the next hundred or so pages, you will find examples of each of these ways of mystery-making. You'll encounter fake news, misunderstandings, fables, bad history and more. You'll see mysteries grow from ordinary events into national sensations. You'll see the roots of some myths stretching back for thousands of years.

You'll also encounter real-life baffling events. Genuine mysteries which, after every explanation is tried, still leave an awkward silence which evades all attempts at providing an answer!

Join me in this book to explore some of Portsmouth's many mysteries. And share your own stories on our *Mysteries of Portsmouth* facebook group, too!

Every story in this book is sourced from histories, newspapers or journals. Some are easily answered - but some remain unanswered to this day.

In any case, it's up to you to decide if they might be true...

...Enjoy!

Matt Wingett,
August 2019

I
ANCIENT MYSTERIES OF PORTSMOUTH

EARLIEST ACCOUNTS OF PORTSMOUTH

Most historians agree, the little Hampshire village of Portchester is the father of the city of Portsmouth. It was already an ancient settlement when the Normans thought the little muddy island of Portsea would be the spot to build a town to guard the harbour mouth.

Portchester's Roman castle (the best preserved example north of the Alps) dates back to the 3rd Century, and was built as part of the Saxon Shore defences designed to protect Britain from marauding Saxon invaders. But even back then, when the Roman fortress of *Portus Adurni* was new, Portchester was already ancient.

So, before we jump into the ancient mysteries and legends of the Portsmouth area, let's look at what we know for sure about the village and castle of Portchester, at the point where it emerges from the mists of myth into history.

PORTCHESTER - HEART OF AN EMPIRE!

Portchester Castle and the rest of the Saxon Shore castles were built somewhere around the year 285 by order of Roman General Marcus Aurelius Carausius.

Carausius started as a Belgian pilot and fighter, but proved so effective a leader of men that he was given command of the *Classis Britannica*, the Roman Fleet that protected the English Channel from pirates. A brilliant sea fighter, he had impressive success in quelling Saxon and Frankish piracy in the English Channel, both in Gaul and Britain.

With success came rivalry, and rumours soon began to circulate that Carausius waited for Saxon pirates to make raids before engaging them - and helped himself to their stolen treasure.

Whether this was the result of jealous gossip or true, in the year 286, Roman Emperor Diocletian sentenced Carausius

to death. This was a tactical error. When Carausius heard his recall to Rome was to face execution, he declared Britain a separate empire equal to Rome, drove off imperial attacks and began to spread his influence in northern Gaul.

Secure and independent behind his forts, Carausius set about creating an empire to rival Rome. To boost his fledgling state's credibility, the coins of his new empire were minted from higher quality bullion than Rome's, and he put literary references on them to assert his claim to cultural superiority. He styled himself "Emperor of the North," and it's believed most of England and Wales was under his rule. Evidence of his influence has been found as far north as Carlisle.

This early attempt at British independence came to a bloody end soon after his betrayal in 293 by his treasurer, Allectus. The usurper was no soldier and Britain soon fell back under Roman Imperial rule.

Carausius's story is a fascinating early true history... but there are also many myths about Portchester and Portsmouth that may or may not contain a grain of truth. These legends include bloodthirsty betrayals, murder, a giant, the Holy Grail... and even King Arthur himself!

FERREX AND PERREX

Ancient chronicler and recorder of generally unreliable histories, Geoffrey of Monmouth, wrote in his *History Of The Kings Of Britain* in the 1200s that the original British name for Portchester was *Caer Peris*. He tells the following story about how it got its name:

Around 491 BCE, two brothers lived in bitter rivalry. They were the sons of King Sisil "The Fox", who founded the town of Silchester. Sisil was so successful a leader that he rose to the level of supreme chieftain of the southern part of Britain.

Though he was a great king, he wasn't able to control the jealousy between his two sons, Ferrex and Perrex. After he died, they went to war to gain control of their father's lands. After losing a fierce battle, Ferrex (his mother's favourite) was forced to retreat to Gaul where he raised an army and returned to fight his brother again. Things went terribly wrong for Ferrex - and this time Perrex killed him.

Geoffrey of Monmouth tells us Perrex set about founding the fortified town where Roman Portchester Castle would

later stand - the name *Caer Peris* meaning *Perrex's Castle*.

The story does not end here, however. Perrex's mother, Idon, enraged at the fate of her favourite son, stole into Perrex's room while he slept, and with the help of her maidens "cut him all in pieces."

This is not a recommended model for motherhood.

GURGUNTUS AND BELINE

Another mythical beginning to Portchester is told by a later historian, John Stow, who attributes the founding of the fortifications to Gurguntus, the son of Beline in the year 375 BCE. However, Stow also says the same thing happened in Norwich with the same people in the same year - so he might have got a little muddled.

Nothing much more is offered about this supposed origin of the castle - however, it should be said there are many archaeological remains dating back to the pre-Christian era in the area. So, whether there's any truth in these early myths or not, there was definitely early settlement here, and defensive structures stood in Portchester long before the Romans came.

Who built those early defences remains unknown.

SHAKESPEARE'S CYMBELINE

(OR CYMBELINE'S SONS, ANYWAY)

The next mention Geoffrey of Monmouth makes of *Caer Peris* brings us to the First Century, during the period the Romans were still quelling the troublesome and rebellious Britons, after their invasion in the year 43.

This account involves a young British king whose father was one King Cunobelinus - otherwise known as Cymbeline to anyone who knows their Shakespeare.

"After the death of Cymbeline," writes Geoffrey, "the government of Britain fell to Guiderius, his son. This prince refused to pay tribute to the Romans, for which reason Claudius, Emperor of Rome, marched against him."

The story goes that Hamo, the commander of the Roman forces made an attack on *Caer Peris*, and "began to block up the gate with a wall," probably with the view of starving the inhabitants into surrender.

In the fighting that followed, Guiderius was killed.

This was not the end of the matter. Guiderius's brother, Arviragus, mightily enraged, took command of the Britons, who fought so desperately under him that they drove the

Romans back to their galleys.

Once again, the story didn't end there. Later, when the Britons had departed, Claudius assaulted the fortification once more, and this time took it for Rome.

The rest, as they say, is history.

Literally.

KING ARTHUR AND THE INVASION OF PORTSMOUTH

Another ancient story about the defence of Portsmouth takes us fully into the realms of Arthurian Romance.

Many of the early King Arthur stories tell of the time when Britain was being invaded by Saxon tribes, just after the Romans left her shores to protect the Empire from increasing attack at the centre.

The reality or otherwise of King Arthur is hotly debated. Whether Arthur was an imaginary folk hero spoken about around British campfires to keep up morale hundreds of years later, a soldier who fought in the battles between the Britons and the Saxons, a half-remembered sun god (the twelve battles he fights that push him further west, his death, disappearance in the west and subsequent promised return are perhaps an echo of the twelve months of the year, sunset and sunrise) or something else, isn't important for the purposes of this book. The stories that have been woven around this most enigmatic of figures who stands on the mythical side of the border between legend and history are as rich in story detail as he is elusive in fact. And what's great about Arthur is the sheer amount of stories he has inspired.

Tracking him from soldier, through war leader, to king and finally emperor of a vast land, the legends about Arthur are increasingly embellished by the romance writers of the Middle Ages.

The first description of Arthur as "emperor" is found in connection with Portsmouth. It's in a poem dedicated to the death of another Celtic hero of Welsh literature. The poem is called *Geraint mab Erbin*, that is, *Geraint son of Erbin*.

Geraint was a popular figure associated with southwestern Britain and South Wales during the Arthurian period, which was the 6th Century. In later years, he became famous for an entirely fictional Welsh language romance known in English as *Geraint and Enid*, which mimics a similar 12th Century poem by French mediaeval poet Chrétien de Troyes.

But Geraint had been around in literature long before this romance, and the far older poem speaks of him as a real person. Thus, *Geraint son of Erbin* might well be a true lament for the death of a British hero killed in battle, in which truth and Arthurian myth mingle.

The location of the battle is given as *Llongborth*, meaning "haven of ships", which writers and historians have identified with Langport in Somerset - or with Portsmouth Harbour. The poem tells of the slaying of the Celtic prince Geraint by the Saxons.

Could the ancient poem really be Portsmouth-related? Is there any other evidence of a battle during the 6th Century in Portsmouth, in which a British hero was killed?

Interestingly enough, the *Anglo-Saxon Chronicles* also mention the invasion of Portsmouth in the year 501:

Port and his two sons, Bieda and Mægla, came with two ships to Britain at the place which is called Portsmouth. They soon landed, and slew on this spot a young Briton of very high rank.

Is it possible that the *Anglo-Saxon Chronicles* actually tell of the death of that same young prince mentioned in the poem *Geraint mab Erbin* ?

And if Geraint, a supposed figure of legend was real, is it possible there *was* an Arthur after all..?

Who can say? But this is exactly how legends arise: with a hope that something just *might* be true!

ANCIENT BURIALS & BRUTAL DEATHS ON PORTSDOWN HILL

Staying on the theme of slain ancient warriors, it's worth noting that at the top of Portsdown Hill as you head east toward the cutting where the A3(M) now slices through the chalk cliffs at the Havant end, around the year 1816 a tantalising discovery was made by labourers. Local historian Lake Allen tells the story in his 1817 *History of Portsmouth*:

Some labourers being employed in quarrying chalk during the month of September last, accidentally broke into a tumulus situated on the South side of the hill near the telegraph. The form of it appeared to be a parallelogram, extending East and West about 100 feet, in breadth about 20 feet, and in height 6 feet. In this tumulus or barrow were discovered the remains of twelve bodies, some placed in cists, others laid only on the surface of the chalk, and covered by heaping the surrounding soil on them. The skeleton that was last discovered occupied a grave distinct from the others, but evidently too short for the stature of the person interred; loose flags were placed on it, their ends resting on the chalk. The radius and ulna were laid across the frame; the latter was the only bone entire, and was rather shorter than that of a well proportioned man. The occipital bone bore marks of petrifaction, and at the juncture of the temporal with the parietal bone, on the right side, was found inserted an iron head of a spear.

"Is it possible that the spearhead found in this body was none other than the one used by Port to slay Geraint mab Erbin..? A man in a tomb, killed by an iron spear, hurriedly buried under loose flagstones by a vanquished army... is it too much of a stretch of the imagination to at least *wish* it were true?"

This way of linking the dots to make a picture that fits unconnected facts is *so* tempting...

And it's one of the ways myths are made!

"BEVIS'S GRAVE"

The ancient archaeological site with mythical connotations described by Lake Allen still lies in the fields north of the Portsdown Hill Road. It is a scheduled ancient monument and is known by the title of "Bevis's Grave".

Although the site was apparently used for Saxon-era burials, this giant long barrow pre-dates the Saxons by a long margin, being between 4,500-5,500 years old.

Bevis's Grave more accurately measures 88m long by 25m wide with ditches to north and south. These days, it is largely buried, with only a part of it rising about half a metre above the ground. Part of an antler, probably the remains of a pick, was excavated from the ditches, along with sherds of late Neolithic and Bronze Age pottery.

The whole area along the crest of Portsdown Hill is rich in archaeology. Nearby is an area of early medieval burials, including two Saxon burials and eighty Christian graves dating from the 8th and 9th Centuries. It is strange to think, as you take your dog for a walk or drive down into Bedhampton that you are surrounded by so many relics of the deep, distant past!

So, that name, *Bevis's Grave*... Where is it from? Who was Bevis? And how did this barrow on a hill get to be his grave?

In fact, Bevis is a much later addition to the long history of this ancient site. He was a mediaeval knight from a Middle English romance called *Sir Bevis of Hampton*, which was written around 1324.

Here are the bare bones of the fictional tale:

Bevis is the son of Guy, count of Hampton (aka Southampton). Guy's young wife, a daughter of the King of Scotland is unhappy in marriage and asks a former lover, Devoun, Emperor of Germany, to kill her husband. He happily sends an army to oblige and Guy is murdered in a forest. Fearful that their ten-year-old son Bevis will seek revenge, she decides that he, too, must die.

Saved by a faithful tutor, the young Bevis is later sold to pirates. After many adventures, Bevis ends up at the court of King Hermin, which is situated either in Egypt or Armenia - the writer is a bit vague on the details of where, exactly. Whilst he's here, Bevis is involved in numerous exploits, including the defeat of Ascapart, a legendary giant from English folklore, and falls in love with the king's daughter, Josiane.

The king, concerned for his daughter, sends Bevis on a mission to deliver a sealed letter to King Bradmond of Damascus. Bevis, not realising the letter requests Bradmond to execute him, duly delivers it. He is imprisoned, escapes, finally wreaks vengeance on his stepfather and claims his inheritance. However, he is then separated from Josiane, and both are forced into false marriages, until they are finally reunited at last.

Phew! It would make a great movie.

So, there it is. Though the barrow's original inhabitant is long forgotten, a wonderful story has filled it with fresh life - which is one of the great things myths and legends do!

ROMANO-CELTIC TEMPLE, HAYLING ISLAND

Heading east and south from Bevis's grave you go through Havant and across a short bridge to reach Hayling Island.

Few people know that in North Hayling in the First Century there once stood an ancient Romano-Celtic temple. The only clues to the site's existence are the post holes and foundations for the buildings that once stood there.

This explains why services are not currently being offered for pagan tourists.

Nevertheless, archaeologists have pieced together what the building looked like: a circular tower about 9 metres in diameter surrounded by a more-or-less square outer enclosure. The whole structure would have been roofed, though perhaps the tower might have protruded further into the sky than the surrounding building. The tower was accessed through a porch and doorway from the enclosure, and at its centre was a pit, which was found to contain artefacts, coins and other items associated with pagan rituals.

The exact role of the priest and the identity of the gods or goddesses worshipped on Hayling will probably never be known. It's likely that people came to worship from the surrounding area, just as they do when they go to church today. Perhaps handfastings and festivals were held there - as well as it being a place to go when you needed to get the gods on your side.

The site of the temple is in Towncil Field. Though there is nothing to see there, quite a few learned papers have been written about it.

If you're curious, have a search online to find out more!

HAYLING ISLAND: HOME OF THE HOLY GRAIL?

Some legends say the most famous figure of the Roman era once visited Britain: none other than Jesus Christ himself.

Even better, a theory I stumbled over in a pamphlet some time ago from the pen of local author Victor Pierce Jones connects Christ's supposed visit to Britain with the fabulous idea that the Holy Grail is buried at Hayling Island!

Legend says the Holy Grail is the magical cup Christ's disciples drank from at the Last Supper. His blood was later collected in it at the Crucifixion, and it is supposed to bestow mystical powers of renewal. In *Glastonbury Myth or Southern Mystery?* Jones argues that "Jesus travelled from the Holy Land as a youth, lived on the south coast and was given a cup when he departed." This cup later became the Holy Grail, which Joseph of Arimathea brought back to Britain after Christ's death, "returning it to his first disciples and friends" who lived in Havant, of all places, which Jones assures us is the "real site of Avalon".

Jones asks: "Did Merlin live at My Lord's Pond, on Hayling Island? Did King Arthur find Excalibur at Havant? Was the Holy Grail found by Benedictine monks and a Knight Templar on Hayling - and is it still hidden there?"

Along the way, the author includes some of the sites and characters already mentioned in this book. As well as King Arthur, Bevis gets a look-in, as does William the Conqueror and countless duplicitous Glastonbury monks. Argued with a passion, it is quite joyous and, I think, a bit bonkers.

But that's just me. The construction of the argument is a work of art, and for seekers after mysteries, it's a slim volume with which to fill your boots!

PAUL'S GROVE

Another local legend connected to a biblical visitor provides the name of what is now a large housing estate near Wymering - that is, Paulsgrove. The story goes that the Paul in question is none other than St Paul, who is said to have arrived in Britain to spread the Word in his travels after his conversion to Christianity. One account tells how he planted his staff in the ground and it miraculously flourished, growing into a grove of trees. Whether there was once a sacred grove here, perhaps venerated by the local Celts is not known, though it's possible. That said, if it did once exist, the bulldozers moved in long ago.

A less exciting explanation for Paulsgrove's name is shown in old maps, where it was written *Pals Grave* - Pal being the name of an ancient Saxon chieftain or king.

It's a little less mysterious than the other story.

I know which one I prefer!

GHOST OF BEHEADED COUNTESS!

There are many ghost stories associated with Portsmouth and its surroundings. Here's one from Warblington, which is on the coast just north of Hayling Island. This one is a guaranteed spine-tingler based on hard fact:

Five hundred years ago at Warblington, by the ever-moving waters of Langstone Harbour once stood a magnificent castle, of which only a few vestiges remain, and on whose ruins in the 18th Century, a farmhouse was built. In its heyday it was one of the chief guesthouses of the Earls of Salisbury. The ghost that haunts the site is that of the unhappy Margaret, Countess of Salisbury, who once lived here in great state, dividing her time between Warblington and Lordington Manor, near Racton, which was commissioned by her husband, Richard.

Their children included Cardinal Reginald Pole, who was the last Catholic Archbishop of England during the period of the Reformation, in which Henry VIII came into direct conflict with Rome. Cardinal Pole was unbending in his attitudes to Henry and strongly criticised him for his divorce from Catherine of Aragon. He also warned against his marriage to Anne Boleyn. Sensing danger from the king's growing impatience with him, Cardinal Pole went into exile in France, where he finally denounced Henry to the other princes of Europe.

The ruthless tyrant Henry VIII attempted to assassinate Pole, but when this failed, he avenged himself by having Pole's family arrested. His mother, Margaret, Countess of Salisbury, was imprisoned in the Tower of London for two and a half years on trumped-up political charges. She was finally beheaded at Tower Hill in 1541, the last surviving issue from the direct male bloodline of the Plantagenet kings of England. Only one family member survived, her son Geoffrey Pole, who, like his brother, fled into exile in Europe. The Pole family was thus completely destroyed as a dynasty by their merciless king.

Accounts of Margaret's execution tell of a grisly end.

On the morning of 27 May 1541, in front of a crowd of 150 people, Lady Pole was led to the scaffold where she was expected to say a few pious words and submit to her fate. But the 67-year-old had no intention of going quietly. She refused to kneel or lay her head on the block, and told the executioner he would have to strike her head off where she stood. Guards roughly took her resisting form to the block, where the executioner raised his axe... and - thrown off his stroke by her defiance - swung the blade and struck her in the shoulder.

In agony, Lady Pole jumped up shrieking, gushing blood into her white hair. The executioner chased her, wildly swinging his axe. It took eleven bloody blows before she finally died. Legend in the Tower of London says that on the anniversary of her death, her ghost is seen in the night, her white hair streaming with blood from her many wounds - forever pursued by her phantom executioner.

After the destruction of the Pole family, the estate was forfeited to the Crown, and a few years later, Thomas Cromwell had Warblington Castle demolished. What was left of it then fell into decay and farmhouses were built over part of it.

A local story tells of a different sighting of a spirit at the site. It says that the ghost of the beheaded and tragic Countess Margaret Pole haunts the ruins, as she mourns the passing of her lost life and her magnificent home.

How the mighty may fall!

Please note - There are many more ghost stories to come in the pages of this book, but first, let me tell you about the Lost Lands around Portsmouth...

2
LOST LANDS

ATLANTIS, MU, THE GREAT FLOOD... AND... PORTSMOUTH?

A common story that appears in many ancient myths is that of lands lost to the sea. From myths of Atlantis, Lemuria, the Lost Continent of Mu and numerous other stories, the idea of sunken landscapes haunts the mythic imagination.

Legends that speak of lands under the waters include the story of the Deluge in the biblical fable of Noah, the Flood in the *Epic of Gilgamesh*, the Chinese Great Flood myth, and even Javan stories of the Queen of the Underworld having a palace under the sea. All these stories must come from somewhere.

Of course, real lands are lost in real life. Just so with the Ancient Egyptian city of Heracleion, only mentioned in a handful of ancient texts, but which was spotted beneath the sea in 1933 by an RAF pilot as he flew over Abu Qir Bay.

The city of Heracleion collapsed into the water thanks to earthquakes and soil liquefaction, and by the 8th Century was completely lost. It has only been properly explored since 1999 when a sub-aqua archaeological expedition began surveying the area.

With the Earth's climate in a period of change, it looks likely there will be many more lands lost to the sea.

It happened before when the Earth warmed.

Doggerland, the land bridge that once linked south-eastern England to mainland Europe during the last Ice Age now lies at the bottom of the North Sea. Evidence of settlement and forests have been discovered under the water, with the skulls of woolly mammoths among the many animal bones trawlermen have landed over the years.

Who knows, maybe one day future archaeologists will marvel at a submerged brick house beneath the sea as they explore your sunken front room - and wonder *who once lived here?*

15

HAYLING ISLAND - THE LOST BELLS

Whilst the Portsmouth area has no grand claim to lost cities, it does have its story of a lost land - and it is more or less true.

The story of the Lost Bells of Hayling Island tells how on certain nights the peal of a sunken church can still be heard ringing under the water.

Local journalist Bob Hind described the story he heard as a boy in the 1960s:

When I was at school we were told that hundreds of years ago Hayling Island was overcome by a massive flood.

The small community with the church to the south of the island was flooded by a massive tide which came in but never went out. The schoolmaster even told us a spooky tale. Apparently legend has it that the church bell could be heard when the tide came and went for a long time after it was covered by the sea.

This local legend definitely has a basis in truth. It's estimated that before the 1200s, Hayling Island was about twice the size of the island today. Over the centuries increasing areas were overcome by coastal erosion, possibly due to deforestation. During the winter of 1324-5, the church of Hayling Priory which once stood at Eastoke was inundated, along with a large part of the settlement.

All this is well-recorded fact. There really is a sunken church out there under the waves, just as Bob Hind said.

The question is: where?

Various fishing charts and admiralty maps show an area in the Solent called Church Rocks. It is one and a quarter miles south from the current shoreline of Eastoke. Could it be the site of the old church? As yet, no evidence has been unearthed to say it could be, but that doesn't mean to say that one day it won't be!

And what of that bell supposedly ringing as the tide came in and went out?

Long before the inundation, the administrators of the Priory realised they were going to have to abandon the church to the waves. Construction of a new one was well underway when the old one finally disappeared beneath the sea. Archaeological evidence suggests that a stone Saxon cross was even moved from the old site to act as a point of focus for worship in the new one. Is it likely that the locals would have brought this, but left an expensive bell behind?

Probably not -

But that said, the sound of a bell ringing more than a mile out to sea...

...That is too ap-*pealing* as far as local mysteries go!

PETRIFIED FOREST

Hayling's lost lands don't stop there, however. Some years ago, a far more ancient relic was found in the water off the island by Havant Borough Council's sea defence group: nothing less than the petrified remains of a forest!

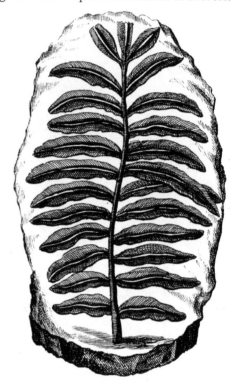

The ancient trees of that submarine land were not lost to the sea a mere few centuries back - in fact carbon dating shows they grew 6,400 years ago, in wide, lush valleys south of where the current shoreline ends.

Going even further back to the last Ice Age 10,000 years ago, global sea levels were as much as 120 metres lower than they are today. Portsmouth and Hayling were then high plains looking down on the valleys below, perhaps a little like Portsdown Hill looks over Portsmouth and Hayling today. There was no Solent sea, but the ancient Solent River had the River Frome as its source, and was fed by tributaries from the higher lands of what are now Portsea Island, Hayling, Fareham and the rest of the modern south coast.

Some of those tributary rivers still exist - the Avon, the Test, the Itchen and the Medina once all fed the ancient long-lost Solent River. Viewed from what is now Hayling Island, streams would have dropped down through broad valleys as they rushed to feed it.

Archaeological remains show that Langstone Harbour was another high plain, with open grassland and woods where people came to collect flint to make tools, hunt and graze sheep and cattle.

To think: long before the hovercraft, it might have been a simple walk and a wade or a short swim to reach the Isle of Wight from Portsmouth!

Of the people who lived here and the lives they led, the beliefs they shared, the battles they fought and the creatures they farmed or hunted, nothing is known.

All now is covered by the murky waters of the Solent, which guards its secrets beneath thick layers of silt.

GATCOMBE - THE LOST HAVEN

From stories of lost lands, to a story of a lost sea.

Maps of Portsmouth from before the 17th Century show a large inlet of water opposite Hayling island on the east side of Portsea Island. Entered via Langstone Harbour it used to be a large and capacious haven..

This was Gatcombe Haven. Roughly speaking, its shoreline stretched along today's Airport Service Road, down Dundas Lane and then across to what is now the Great Salterns Recreation Ground. What's amazing is when you overlay modern maps on old ones showing Gatcombe Haven, the shape of of the old bay is still easily seen in the undeveloped parts of that part of Portsmouth today.

Perhaps Great Salterns should not be in this book at all. It's no mystery as to why the Haven disappeared. Production of salt through evaporation in salt works, or salterns, was an industry that had gone on in the harbour since before the Romans came, and as the industry became more developed and the haven saw increased use, the haven was steadily reclaimed for industrial use.

In 1666 Richard Alchorne had 100 acres of salt pits dug and began to produce a more refined salt at the Great Salterns works. Gatcombe Haven filled up steadily over the centuries.

The last vestiges of the old bay that once bit into this part of Portsea Island were finally filled in after World War Two, when a period of rubbish dumping meant the land had to be improved.

Gatcombe Haven is not a mystery, then, but it is a reminder that the land under our feet is constantly changing, and that where we drive today might once have been the place where a ship sailed or a saltworker toiled out his hours, labouring to make salt crystals that would preserve meat eaten by the Royal Navy's sailors in the furthest corners of the world!

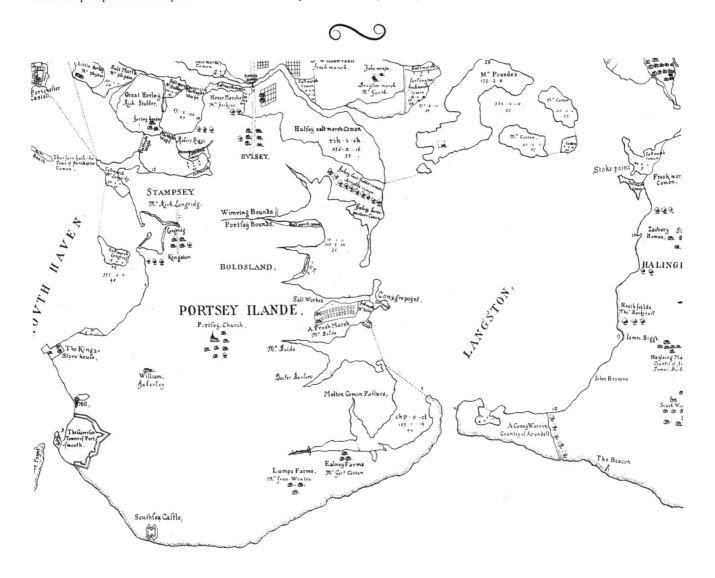

3
FLYING SAUCER MADNESS!

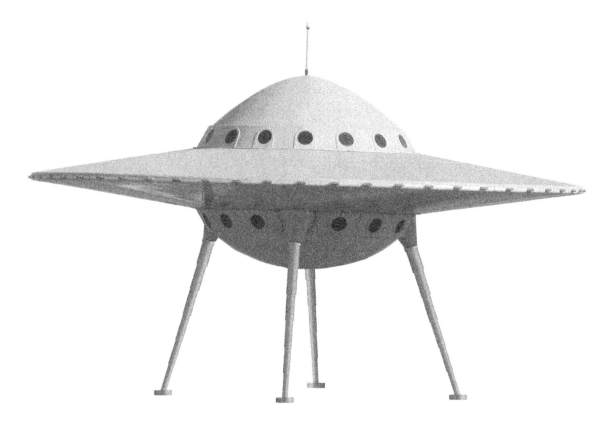

UFOS -
HOW IT ALL BEGAN

From ancient lands to the thoroughly modern mystery of UFOs, with which Portsmouth has a special connection. But before we look at local facts, let's recap the history of the Flying Saucer Phenomenon.

It all began in the USA. A few minutes before 3.00 pm on June 24th 1947, American pilot Kenneth Arnold, flying on a business trip, saw a bright flashing light, looking like reflected sunlight in the sky, at about 9,200 feet over Washington State.

He checked for aircraft nearby and found the airspace clear. Thirty seconds later, a line of bright lights flashed in the distance. Arnold wondered if they might be reflections in the cockpit and assured himself they were outside the plane. Seeing these Unidentified Flying Objects were flying in a long chain formation, Arnold at first wondered if they were a flock of geese, or a new type of jetplane.

The UFOs quickly approached Mount Rainier, appearing dark in profile against the mountain's bright white snowfield. Arnold said sometimes they looked flat, making them practically invisible. He estimated these extremely agile disc-like objects making sharp banks and turns in the air to be the size of a DC-4 airliner, and travelling somewhere between 1200 and 1700 miles per hour.

In later interviews he compared their shape to saucers... And so, the phrase "flying saucer" was born.

MENTAL ILLNESS

This sighting in the USA started the UFO craze that swept the world. Over the decades it would go on to encompass stories of alien abductions, inter-species sex experiments, and conspiracies of stolen alien technology being held in Area 51, the secret US airforce base in the Nevada Desert.

In those early days, some witnesses were accused of lying or hallucination, some of attention-seeking, and others of mental illness...

...But there were enough level-headed witnesses to leave a question mark over these strange phenomena, meaning reports *had* to be taken seriously.

INVESTIGATIONS BEGIN

Working on several theories - including the idea that a terrestrial hostile power had developed a new superjet, or that these *really were* visitations from potentially hostile aliens - the US military began to investigate.

At the height of Cold War paranoia in the US, some argued these alien visitors were part of a Communist invasion. Communism, US patriots argued, was so opposed to "normal" human life that it must be from another planet. Others theorised the whole phenomenon was created by the US Government to hide tests of experimental aircraft.

Conspiracy theories proliferated, in much the way they do today on social media.

MUCH EARLIER UFO OVER PORTSMOUTH...

This was not the first time mysterious flying objects had caused worldwide hysteria. Nearly 40 years before the outbreak of Flying Saucer sightings, Portsmouth had already been part of an earlier wave UFO scare. An article in *The Guardian* of 27th November 1913 announced:

During the past week, scores of persons in various parts of England have convinced themselves that they have seen an airship in the night sky. Most of the reports agree that two bright lights appeared close together, hovered in the air for a time, and then rapidly disappeared. Some of the observers add that they heard the droning of an engine. The reports come from several places on the east coast and also Portsmouth. Based on these facts suggestions are now being made in many quarters and positive assertions in others that German airships have travelled each night over England.

Portsmouth was thus involved in the *Phantom Airship Panic* that swept America, New Zealand and Europe between 1909 and 1913. No solution was given for these sightings, but in the mounting political tension between Britain and Germany, the article sought to defuse anxiety by arguing it was not proven that these were German airships.

Striking a cautious note, the *Guardian* asked why a craft making a secret visit to Britain would have its lights on, and pointed out how difficult it is for a non-expert to identify a dirigible at night.

It finished by observing that many of the sightings had been made when Venus was sinking toward the horizon, and suggested people had actually seen a star or planet.

To this day, no-one knows what these Phantom Airships were. But, since stars tend not to have engines, and dirigibles do not move at high speed, could it *really* have been a German spy mission? Was *The Guardian* right that it was just a star in the sky? Or was it something else entirely?

The mystery remains unanswered.

SUPER-FAST SAUCER

So, we come to the Cold War period. After the 1947 Keith Arnold case in the USA, a rash of Flying Saucer sightings occurred - some over Portsmouth.

On September 26th 1947, The *Hampshire Telegraph* ran an article headlined *Thinks He Saw A "Flying Saucer"*. It reported that Mr J M Carney of Havant Road, Cosham "saw an object travelling across the sky" which he said could only be described as a "flying saucer".

Carney described the object as "glistening gold" in the sun while it headed west in a straight line at "tremendous speed". It was moving "as fast as you can turn your head," he went on, and added he thought at first it might have been a shooting star, "but it had no trajectory and I was able to watch it run out of sight." Carney was emphatic about what he saw, and asked if others had seen it.

Sightings across the country abounded, causing a minor flurry of interest in newspapers but little more... until something strange happened in the skies over Portsmouth.

FIRST OFFICIAL UK SIGHTING

On the afternoon of the 1st of June 1950 at 14.30 while flying at 20,000 feet, a Gloster Meteor pilot flying out of RAF Tangmere reported passing a flying saucer illuminated with bright lights. The object was "shining, revolving, and disc-like" and "flying eastwards over the Portsmouth area."

RAF Tangmere contacted the radar station at RAF Wartling, Sussex, to discover if it had seen the object. The duty controller confirmed that he and three radar operators had tracked it independently on radar screens, travelling at 1,300 - 1,650 knots, first approaching and then receding from the station.

This clear sighting by a trained pilot over Britain's premier naval base, where new military technology is developed, fitted and trialled on ships and aircraft, became the first UFO sighting to be officially recognised by the UK military.

In response to the report and several others that had come in, the MOD set up an investigation group it dubbed the FSWP - that is, the *Flying Saucer Working Party*.

As well as having a really cool name, the FSWP produced the MOD's first official study into UFOs. Their report the following year concluded that the phenomena could all be answered by terrestrial explanations. In the case of the RAF Tangmere event, it concluded that there was a ten minute discrepancy between the visual sighting by the Meteor pilot and that of the radar station. Two other RAF sightings were dismissed in a similar manner.

The report noted that during the summer and autumn of 1950, the Press had given considerable publicity to reports of alleged sightings of luminous bodies travelling at high speed, usually after dark, but occasionally in daylight. It claimed to have investigated them, only to draw the same conclusion in each case: that none was a sighting of extra-terrestrial craft.

PHOTOGRAPHIC EVIDENCE?

One Portsmouth event in this spate of sightings was reported on 3rd August 1950 in an article in the *Portsmouth Evening News* entitled *Did They Snap A Flying Saucer?* It told how Mr D W Thompson of Elson Road, Gosport believed he had taken a photograph of a flying saucer "flashing mysteriously past" over Gilkicker Point at about 6pm.

He and a friend, R J Phillips were out taking photographs, when Thompson attempted to take a shot of hovering seagulls. On developing the film, he discovered a "strange object" in the sky.

At first Thompson thought it might be a secret jet plane,

but closer examination made him think that the unidfentified object "resembles the descriptions given by eye-witnesses of the flying saucer."

What this object was, if anything, remains a mystery. Unfortunately, no photo was published with this report.

MORE FLYING SAUCER SIGHTINGS

In the *Hampshire Telegraph and Post*, of August 4th, 1950, another UFO case appeared:

Mrs E Brockett, of 23 Outram Road, Southsea, says she saw a flying saucer over Portsmouth about 8. a.m. on Tuesday.

"It was just before the end of the eight o'clock news that I saw a flying saucer going towards Hayling Island," she told a reporter. "It was round and silvery, and was travelling fairly slowly. Did anyone else see it?"

There was no independent confirmation of this sighting, but it was typical of the many that occurred throughout the country during this period.

ASTRONOMER ROYAL WADES IN

By the early 1950s, the flying saucer craze was in full swing. Perhaps to allay growing public concern, on 2nd January 1951, the *Portsmouth Evening News* ran an article by Astronomer Royal, Sir Harold Spencer Jones, who with steady confidence strove to demolish news of flying saucer sightings and theories of alien visitations.

His article, entitled *Those Martian Bees Must Be Busy*, commented disdainfully that because of the varied nature of reports of mysterious saucer-like objects in American investigations "it is quite clear that they cannot all relate to the same type of object or phenomenon."

He added with grating superiority:

"It seems to have become common in the United States to call anything seen in the sky which is at all out of the ordinary a 'flying saucer'."

Later, Spencer Jones cast doubt on the descriptions provided of sightings because witnesses generally *agreed* that UFOs make no sound, never land, never take off and that they always disappear into the sky or over the ocean.

This was a strange argument to make.

Whereas previously Spencer Jones had complained that these sightings were all too *different* from each other to be taken seriously, now they were *all too similar!*

LOCH NESS MONSTER AND SECRET WEAPONS

After this, Spencer Jones proclaimed UFO sightings to be essentially the result of mass hysteria, like sightings of the Loch Ness Monster.

He dismissed suggestions that UFOs might be U.S. secret weapons, pilotless planes, or guided missiles undergoing trials, because that had "been officially denied".

Then, having thus argued that the US governments doesn't keep secret weapons secret, in the next sentence he dismissed the possibility they were secret weapons built by an enemy power *because it would want to keep them secret!*

The article was stylishly written, but fell apart at every sentence.

ALIEN BEES

The writing grew stranger when the Astronomer Royal started attacking the more whacky suggestions from flying saucer advocates, whom, he stated, believed that Martians were in fact two-inch long "super-bees". He sneered: "The Martian insects must be extremely competent engineers: large plants would be needed to construct these objects, capable of such great speeds and so perfect in construction that no mishap ever befalls them."

So, what did the Astronomer Royal believe these flying saucers were?

The usual answers were offered: meteorological balloons, meteors, trains of fire-balls, reflections of sunlight, or shadows thrown by aircraft - until finally Spencer Jones went back to the reason given by *The Guardian* for the Portsmouth UFO of 1913: the planet Venus.

He concluded by saying with great authority:

"Flying-saucers, as such, are in fact a myth."

WOT? MORE SIGHTINGS?

Despite Spencer Jones's best efforts to persuade the public flying saucers didn't exist, sightings continued across the country.

Portsmouth was no exception. On January 6th 1951, four days after the appearance of the Spencer Jones article, the *Portsmouth Evening News* ran the following:

GREEN FLAMES, TOO. Another report of a "flying saucer" comes from Mr. Eric W A D Auckett of Queen Alexandra Hospital, Cosham, who says that on Thursday afternoon at about 2.30 he saw an object travelling at a colossal speed. Green flames were coming from it.

However, Spencer Jones did find an ally in one reader, who professed expertise on flying saucers. A letter to the editor of the *Portsmouth Evening News* on 10th January 1951 agreed that they weren't spaceships, but explained that some "are spent rockets which finally explode or evaporate: others may be long range guided missiles." Some of them, it added authoritatively, were actually secret weapons.

Then the writer, who signed himself "Space Prober" added that some Flying Saucers were actually part of a highly secret satellite project in which a station was at that very moment being built in space...

MANY WITNESSES TO MYSTERY IN SKY

Spencer Jones's attempt at level-headedness, then, did nothing to stop Portsmouth's fascination with UFOs.

A classic sighting headlined *MYSTERY "ROCKET"* appeared in the *Portsmouth Evening News* on November 21st 1952.

It reported that a "huge rocket with a sparkling tail" was seen travelling at high speed in a north-easterly direction at about 6 o'clock in the morning over several places near Portsmouth. It added:

While loading his van at Arctic Road, Cowes at 5.55 this morning, Mr. Peter Butt looked up into the darkened sky.

He saw a green light, with what appeared to be orange-yellow flames coming from behind it. It came from the south-west and disappeared travelling north-east in less than ten seconds.

Mr Butt's first impression was that it was some kind of rocket, but he could not account for the green light. The object made no noise.

Early morning bus travellers in the Leigh Park area also saw "the rocket".

Said one eye witness: "It was going at about 600 mph in a north easterly direction, and was below cloud level. The object was not a jet plane - because we heard no noise. It lit up the dark sky as it went through."

It would seem Royal Astronomer Spencer Jones had plenty more work to do to disprove flying saucers!

AIR MARSHALL REVEALS EXPERIMENTAL FLYING SAUCER PLANE

On 6th May 1953, Air Marshal Sir Robert Saundby KBE, acknowledged the debate raging about UFOs and added an extra piece of information in an article in the *Portsmouth Evening News*. Aircraft makers A V Roe of Canada, he wrote, had developed designs for a ring-shaped aircraft with a central plastic bubble cockpit and a revolutionary engine.

The appearance of this aircraft is strikingly similar to that of the "flying saucer," about which many reports have accumulated, but which no-one has ever captured or even photographed... Avro's design team apparently believe that such a shape is practicable and advantageous for supersonic flight. If they are proved to be right, it will no doubt awaken a new interest in the many and persistent reports of "flying saucers" in our skies.

INTERPLANETARY WARFARE

The Air Marshal was wrong: interest in flying saucers was already wide awake. A string of correspondence in the *Portsmouth Evening News* revealed how for some, flying saucers had become a matter of faith.

Gosport resident Ewart Lander became convinced that someone was interfering in the earth's weather systems, and wrote to the *Portsmouth Evening News* that he believed that

1954's late spring was due to hostile aliens. Another reader, A M Laver, took exception to Lander's alien weathermen.

Lander's reply was fulsome and filled with the kind of thinking that basks in science, without being scientific. He cited previous technological advances that no-one would before have believed possible, such as radio communication and heavier-than-air flight as evidence that things that appear impossible really can happen. It was exactly the same case with controlling the weather, he added.

He warned that weather-controlling technology could divert rain clouds to either nourish or destroy an economy, enabling the controller to kill millions. He urged, with more than a shade of paranoia, "Sinister and evil forces are again attempting to dominate the world: and some of the world's greatest scientists are in their ranks. Is there any doubt that they would hesitate to use any method to achieve their aims?" He pointed to "unprecedented electric storms, deluges, hurricanes and tidal waves" before asking "could these disasters have been produced by man - or other forces of which we have no knowledge?"

The conspiracy theory, it seems, is nothing new!

His letter got short shrift from four readers, each with very different takes on what he'd written. Their letters appeared in the *Portsmouth Evening News*, on June 22nd, 1954. Some appealed to reason and even to Jesus for their counterarguments, while one questioner asked the basic question: since this was the worst summer for 49 years, what had caused the bad weather 50 years ago? Was that also aliens?

Ewart Lander stuck to his guns. Reading his letters in the *Portsmouth Evening News*, I wonder if perhaps he was born too early and would have revelled in the conspiracies to be found on social media today.

His belief in the Martian threat appeared to have grown into an obsession, as his letter to the *Portsmouth Evening News* of July 2nd 1954, revealed:

Sir - Your correspondent "A.S." of Petersfield writes: "Interplanetary warfare may be completely ruled out... the very idea is ludicrous."

Perhaps he could therefore explain why Canada, taking no chances on a surprise Martian invasion, has set up a "flying saucer" look-out post.

It's stated that the reason for this precaution is that Mars is now at the nearest point to the earth for 13 years; furthermore a statement is reported as having been made by an official to the effect that "most 'flying saucer'

reports are made at 18-month intervals, coinciding with the times that the Earth and Mars are in closest proximity."

A NEVER-ENDING STORY

And so, the arguments between those who believed and those who didn't carried on. For those of us today watching the world being swept by bad ideas, deliberate distortions and complete lies, reading reports from these more innocent times reminds us how easily an idea can take hold.

For some, flying saucers were very real, just as for some UFOs are real today. Of the numerous sightings over the years, some have been proven hoaxes, some turned out to be those weather balloons investigators believe crowd the sky - and others really have been sightings of Venus or Jupiter.

But sometimes, in a few cases, something doesn't quite fit. None of the terrestrial explanations fully account for what some people claim to have seen and experienced. It's there the unexplained resides and where theories grow.

The sky above Portsmouth, then, just like the sea around it, is a place of mystery and imagination!

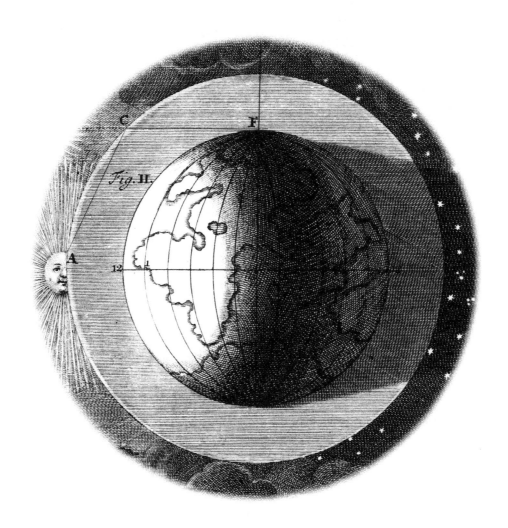

4
THE CURSE OF TUTANKHAMUN

DIGGING FOR CONNECTIONS

An Egyptian curse, a hidden tomb, mysterious deaths and an apparent supernatural attack nearly 50 years on aren't things usually associated with a Portsmouth suburb. But the story of the Curse of Tutankhamun holds all these elements, as well as a striking set of personal tragedies.

The story is of Mr Richard Adamson, who in his retirement in the 1970s lived in Drayton, just north of Portsmouth.

As a younger man, he worked in Egypt as a police officer, and that is where this mystery begins.

In 1922, while patrolling in the Valley of the Kings at Luxor, he noticed some Egyptian locals, who were notorious for tomb-raiding, attempting to cover something over. He

investigated after they left and uncovered a set of steps leading into the ground. Surmising that the gang intended to return later to loot the site, Adamson photographed the location and informed the British archaeologist Howard Carter.

Carter investigated and, much to the dig team's great excitement, the steps turned out to be the entrance to Tutankhamun's tomb. So it was that Adamson found the location of the most famous Egyptian burial chamber the world has ever seen.

Soon after news of the discovery had spread throughout the world, another far darker story began to circulate. It was rumoured that the tomb had a curse upon it, which had killed off the original members of the expedition team.

The story of King Tut's Curse became so established in the public's mind that the sole survivor of the dig, the no-nonsense Adamson, gave an interview to Norwich television in 1970 in which he denounced it.

On 14th January 1970, the *Aberdeen Press and Journal* reported that a strange incident occurred after that fateful interview:

SPOKE
TOO SOON

Soon after saying on television that he did not believe in the legendary death curse of the tomb of Tutankhamen, the last surviving member of the expedition which discovered the tomb in 1922, Mr Richard Adamson of Drayton, Portsmouth, was hurt in a road accident.

This little report appears to show nothing more than an interesting coincidence... However, in an article of 11th January 1982, published nearly 60 years after the discovery of the tomb, the *Liverpool Echo* revealed more details of the crash, in an article called *The Curse of the Boy King*.

The article began:

A WARNING
OF DOOM

Death will come to those who disturb the sleep of the Pharaohs... That was the warning found inscribed in the tomb of the Egyptian boy king Tutankhamun at Luxor when it was opened in February 1923 - for the first time in 3,000 years.

The article described how, before his departure from England for Egypt, expedition leader Lord Carnarvon, received a warning from a friend and mystic predicting his premature death if he went on the archaeological trip.

Stories of Egyptian curses would have been well-known to Carnarvon, who would certainly have heard of the fate of Arthur Weigall, another Egyptologist who apparently succumbed to an Egyptian curse when he brought a sarcophagus back to England.

The article described Weigall's fate: "No sooner had he obtained the coffin than he lost his arm when his gun exploded... The ship in which the coffin was sent home was wrecked. The house in which it was kept was burnt down. The photographer who took a picture of it shot himself. A

lady friend of whom the owner was very fond was lost at sea..." and so the catalogue of disasters went on.

THE CURSE CLAIMS ITS VICTIMS

Despite these portents of doom, the pragmatic 57-year-old Carnarvon pushed on with his plans for the dig.

At first, all appeared to go well. By any standard, the expedition was a success. The tomb of an Egyptian royal, intact and undisturbed by tomb raiders, was the prize archaeologists had sought for centuries in Egypt. Now, thanks to Adamson's sharp eyes, they had found one.

But, the report in the *Liverpool Echo* tells us, the curse soon struck and the list of deaths among the dig team grew long indeed.

The first death occurred in April 1923, when Lord Carnarvon was taken ill. "I feel like hell," he announced when he woke one morning in his hotel room. He lapsed into unconsciousness soon after, and died the same night.

The death was attributed to a mosquito bite, which some noted was in the exact place where there was a blemish on the mummified body of King Tutankhamun.

More bizarrely, at the moment of his father's death, there was a power cut. Carnarvon's son, resting in an adjoining room, said: "The lights suddenly went out all over Cairo. We lit candles and prayed."

Another death at the hotel soon followed. One of the leaders of the expedition, an American archaeologist called Arthur Mace complained of tiredness, went comatose and died before doctors could diagnose what was wrong with him.

Deaths then came thick and fast. George Gould, a close friend of Carnarvon, rushed to Egypt when he was told of his death. He visited Tutankhamun's tomb and went down with a fever that killed him within 12 hours. Archibald Reid, the man who X-rayed Tutankhamun's body, returned home to Britain with exhaustion, and died soon after.

Richard Bethell, Carnarvon's personal secretary on the expedition, was discovered dead in his bed from apparent heart failure. One of the first visitors to the tomb, British Industrialist Joel Wool died from a mysterious fever.

In fact, there were so many deaths that by 1930, there were only two left alive of the original team that had broken into the tomb.

SOLE SURVIVOR

All this, Richard Adamson had gone on television to refute in his 1970 tv interview. He had decided to "explode the myth" of the curse, and told viewers "I don't believe in the myth for one moment".

Then, just after leaving the studio, his taxi was involved in a dramatic crash. The *Liverpool Echo* reveals that it collided with a tractor and that the impact threw Adamson on to the road into the path of a passing lorry. It missed his head by inches. He was extremely lucky to survive.

The next part of the *Echo's* report is chilling:

It was the third time that Adamson, who had been security guard to Lord Carnarvon's expedition, had tried to put paid to the legend. The first time he spoke against it, his wife died within 48 hours. The second time, his son broke his back in a plane crash. After the third occasion, Adamson, recovering in hospital from head injuries, said: "Until now, I refused to believe that there was any connection between the Curse and what happened to my family. But now I am having second thoughts."

This could easily have been one more coincidence in a line of tragic coincidences - but when you join the dots in a certain way, a pattern seems to be revealed...

Curse or coincidence? You decide!

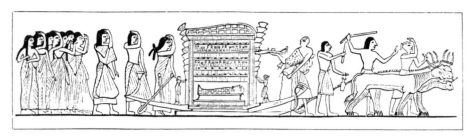

5

INTRODUCING POMPEY GHOSTS

"GHOSTS ARE EVERYWHERE!"

Who doesn't know someone who claims to have seen a ghost - or has seen one themselves?

Who hasn't been spooked on a cold, dark night?

Perhaps you've experienced a feeling of being watched, an inexplicable movement out of the corner of your eye or a sudden cold descending from nowhere that makes your hairs stand on end as you grow inexplicably afraid!

Over the years, countless people in Portsmouth have spoken of ghostly presences and hauntings - but every so often, one story or another becomes so well known, or the phenomena so interesting that they make it into the news.

That's when the debate begins.

Those who claim to to see ghosts will never be convinced by those who say it's illogical. While no amount of logic will shift them from their conviction, those who haven't seen ghosts won't believe without hard scientific evidence.

In the following pages, I don't argue for or against ghosts, but want to share with you some of the ghost-related stories I've found in the papers for your enjoyment, information and delight. Not all the reports I've picked are ghost stories, but all the stories mention ghosts in some way or another. Some writers of these accounts firmly believed, others firmly didn't. But along the way, we see how the fascination with ghosts, and the age-old battle between believers and non-believers, have lasted for what seems like an eternity.

Despite all that arguing, still the mysteries of spirit contact remain a background to many people's lives.

THE TRUTH ABOUT GHOSTS?

On 25th November 1932, an article headlined *Debate On Ghosts* appeared in the *Portsmouth Evening News*, describing how members of the Portsmouth South Junior Imperial League sought to solve the problem of ghosts by debating the motion "That this House believes in ghosts".

Believers pointed to all the ghostly occurrences people claimed to have experienced going back into ancient history.

The other side reasoned scientifically, claiming there was "no point to ghosts", or that they were surely the result of "unwise imbibing or of guilty conscience".

In reply, others again related their own inexplicable ghostly experiences.

It was the age-old debate in a nutshell, leaving believers and sceptics equally convinced of their own views. In all, the Portsmouth South Junior Imperial League were clearly a sceptical bunch, because the *Portsmouth Evening News* announced they "refused to be moved from their materialist frame of mind".

Yet, not everyone in Portsmouth was so certain, and for some, ghosts and spirits were too fascinating and too much fun to ignore.

WISHING YOU A SPOOKY CHRISTMAS

The Victorians were fascinated with spirits, as was reflected in their tradition of publishing Christmas ghost stories. These often included tales of "true hauntings", though such claims of veracity may have been added to give readers an extra frisson.

Other ghost-themed activities were also part of Christmas fun and festivities, and held a massive appeal.

In the *Hampshire Telegraph* for 28th December 1881, among reports of heavy railway traffic into Landport Station, how South Parade Pier was decked with "holly wreaths and bunting for Christmas", announcements that the pantomime *Cinderella* was playing at The Theatre Royal, that variety acts could be enjoyed at Ginnett's Circus and *Red Riding Hood, or the Naughty Wolf* was playing at Myers' American Hippodrome, there appeared the following intriguing headline:

THE AETHERSCOPE AT PORTLAND HALL

Just at this time of the year, when ghost stories are being discoursed with much more than ordinary relish and mystery at most firesides, the "great ghost exhibition" by Messrs. Strange and Wilson at the Portland Hall, Southsea, will be particularly apropos. The effects produced by their combination of the aetherscope, spectroscope and phantoscope are by no means exaggerated when described in the programme by the word "astounding".

The article declared that even the firm disbeliever would be amazed by these ghosts, adding that recent London news reports that "*real* spirits - to use a somewhat paradoxical expression" have been seen, gives "an additional spice of interest to these airy visitants." The show at the Portland Hall gave a "wonderful illusion" of ghosts. "The many changes of figures and scenery effected by this curious application of catoptrics and dioptrics are now seen at their best."

The show included an adaptation of Charles Dickens's *A Christmas Carol* and a farce in which a variety of ghosts entertained with much hilarity. All was accompanied by "a talented company of operatic artistes."

The truth is, whether they were real or not, the Victorians loved their ghosts!

SEASONAL HAUNTS

Spirits came out to play, it seems, when the strange and supernatural phenomena of Christmas (with its tales of angels and divine incarnation and Santa Claus) were also in the air. The most famous Christmas ghost story of Victorian times was Portsmouth-born Charles Dickens's *A Christmas Carol*. This massive international bestseller was just one of four supernaturally-themed books Dickens published over different Christmases.

In the Portsmouth newspapers, a whole page of *Christmas Ghost Stories* appeared in the Christmas Supplement to the *Hampshire Telegraph and Sussex Chronicle* on 22nd December 1894, with such titles as *The Merry Ghosts of Midlow, The Ghost and The Family Bible, Ghosts!* and *A Ghost Says Mass*, alongside a Christmas story set among the Anglo-Saxons, peppered with witchcraft!

These were all ingredients in a rich Christmas mix of articles that included a recipe on how to prepare mincemeat, advice on how to carve meat, a story about Santa Claus and - at the bottom of the page, *A True Ghost Story*.

This last told a supposedly real-life account of how a vicar who didn't believe in ghosts was staying at a country

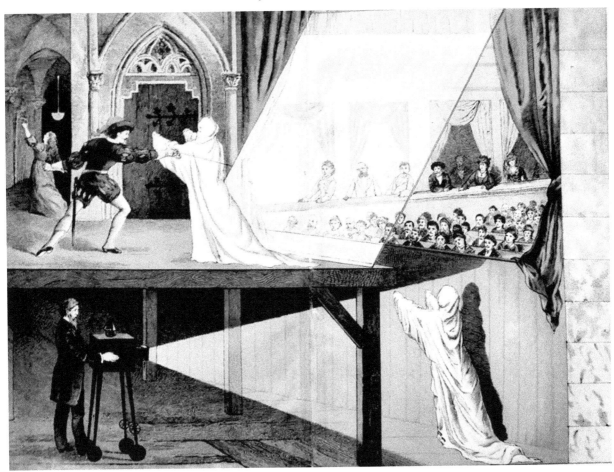

house when he encountered the ghost of a woman who had committed suicide. Its tone was very different from the other stories... yet this too remains a mystery, since no identifying details were given to the location...

So, *true* or *not true*? This one is too vague to investigate!

SPIRITS AND CELEBRITIES IN PORTSMOUTH

Portsmouth-born Charles Dickens was an early member of The Ghost Club, the world's oldest psychical research organisation, founded in 1862. Dickens was clearly inspired by the subject, and wrote 20 ghost stories, while he also included spooky elements in his novels, such as the creepy figure of Miss Haversham in *Great Expectations* in her withered wedding dress, or the strange death in *Bleak House* of Krook, by spontaneous human combustion (which Dickens firmly believed in). His Christmas short story *The Haunted Man* is a recommended spine-tingler, be it Christmas or not!

An interesting follow-up to Charles Dickens's ghostly connection with Portsmouth can be found in a report in the *Portsmouth Evening News* from 4th June 1932. In an article entitled *The Spirit of Dickens*, writer A G Pawsey described how he attended a séance with the medium Leonard B Lilley of 72 Oriel Road, North End, and encountered no fewer than nine different voices.

One such entity was none other than Charles Dickens himself, who, Pawsey reported, caused great interest among the sitters. He added:

Questioned regarding his works, Dickens replied: "My characters were created from the lives of people acting on the greatest stage of all - your world."

Question: "Were you inspired in your works?"

Answer: "Yes, and I am now inspiring others on the earth, and trying to create a better understanding among people."

Question: "Do you rest?"

Answer: "Yes, when I desire. I do not return to your earth each day as you understand time."

Pawsey added:

During his speech, Dickens brought back to life in words one of his characters, Mr Snodgrass from the "Pickwick Papers". After further conversation, Dickens promised to return at a further séance.

Whether the spirit of Dickens made a further appearance, is not reported, though we shall see more of Mr Lilley, later.

CONAN DOYLE AND THE PARANORMAL

During the Victorian period a massive interest in all matters ghostly had been awakened across the world by the Spiritualist Movement, and Britain was no exception.

As well as Charles Dickens, other Victorian celebrities also fascinated by ghostly phenomena included Arthur Conan Doyle. He believed in ghosts, hypnotism, clairvoyance, mediumship, telepathy and just about everything else - up to and including fairies. This was all a far cry from his hero Sherlock Holmes, whom he created while living in The Portsmouth suburb of Southsea in 1886. Conan Doyle's early output included paranormal novels such as *The Mystery of Cloomber* and *The Parasite*, the latter being a novelette about mind control through hypnosis or mesmerism.

Hypnotism was demonstrated in Southsea on the 15th of February 1889 in Portland Hall. The hypnotist, a M Milo De Meyer announced in the *Portsmouth Evening News* on the previous day that "owing to unprecedented success obtained", a "final Séance of MAGNETISM AND NEW HYPNOTISM" would be held. It promised "amusing, interesting and scientific experiments" in which "Ladies and gentlemen among the audience can be magnetised if desired".

The show was in fact "THE GREATEST SENSATION OF THE AGE" it boasted, and stated that "no one should fail to come to this marvellous entertainment... which must be seen to be believed."

Doyle certainly attended just such a demonstration that February, though he was disappointed to find the experiment failed on him.

It wasn't just hypnotism that he investigated while in Portsmouth. For Arthur Conan Doyle, the town was an extremely important place for the development of his belief in ghosts.

When he had come to live in Portsmouth in 1882, he was a convinced materialist, but through meeting members of the Philosophical and Literary Society, he was encouraged to experiment in telepathy. When he became convinced it was real, he moved on to séances, and in 1887 was eventually convinced of the reality of spirit phenomena. On July 2nd 1887, a letter he wrote telling of his conversion was published in *Light* magazine, a journal of the psychical, mystical and occult. He proclaimed:

I believe that it has been found a useful practice among revivalists and other excitable religionists of all types, for each member to give the assembled congregation a description of the manner in which they attained the somewhat vague result known as "finding salvation."

Conan Doyle described how he was converted when he received a message from a medium which was "absolutely inexplicable on any hypothesis except that held by Spiritualists." His investigations in Portsmouth set him on a lifelong path that led him to become the leading Spiritualist figure of the 1920s.

Perhaps the most important moment for Doyle in Portsmouth came when he met his deceased son at a séance in Southsea in the summer of 1919. He wrote of it later:

Then came what to me was the supreme moment of my spiritual experience. It is almost too sacred for full description, and yet I feel that God sends such gifts that we may share them with others. There came a voice in the darkness, a whispered voice, saying. "Jean, it is I." My wife felt a hand upon her head, and cried, "It is Kingsley." I heard the word "Father." I said, "Dear boy, is that you?" I had the sense of a face very near my own, and of breathing. Then the clear voice came again with an intensity and note very distinctive of my son, "Forgive me!" His life was so admirable that I could only think that he referred to our perfectly good-humoured difference about Spiritualism, concerning which, in the bustle of his medical and military life, he really had no chance of forming an opinion, I told him eagerly that I had no grievance of any kind. A large, strong hand then rested upon my head, it was gently bent forward, and I felt and heard a kiss just above my brow. "Tell me, dear, are you happy?" I cried. There was silence, and I feared he was gone. Then on a sighing note came the words, "Yes, I am so happy."

GHOSTS FROM QUEEN ANNE'S TIMES AND SIR WALTER BESANT

Another Portsmouth-born writer, Sir Walter Besant, also believed in ghosts. Besant wrote close to 50 novels and was the founder of The Society of Authors, the organisation that today looks after authors' rights. Now largely forgotten, Besant was compared with Dickens in his day, and indeed, Arthur Conan Doyle praised him in his early writing, and attended a gala dinner held in his honour.

The *Hampshire Telegraph* of 22nd August 1891 reported Besant's accounts of ghost sightings as follows:

The first 'figure' I ever saw was about six o'clock on an evening in September. I had been writing up to the last moment of daylight; it became too dark for me to see any longer, and I knocked off; as I turned from the window I became aware that a female figure was in the room; it made no sign, but it moved about noiselessly. As I looked it disappeared. I was then living as a bachelor in chambers, and my outer door was closed, so that nobody could be in the room except myself.

Another experience, and a far more singular one, was this. I was travelling in Northumberland. The day I had spent in driving over a wild and lonely moor to a village situated in the midst of it - a village built round the quadrangle of what had been a monastery. There was the old gate left; part of the buildings; part of the wall; the quiet village enclosed by the old wall; the convent chapel, now the parish church; there were only two or three hundred people living here; outside ran and babbled the trout stream with its high bank covered with bushes and brambles and wild flowers. All round stretched the moor.

At the inn, where I took some tea or something, they talked to me about the past; the place was filled with echoes of the past; whispers and voices were heard at night; things had been seen in the bedrooms. A wonderful place; nowhere else in England is there a more wonderful place.

I drove back and spent the evening alone in my inn, reading certain books of the Queen Anne time, and at eleven o'clock went off to bed. My room was a very old room, and the inn itself was at least three hundred years old. All this is introduction in order to show you why the thing that I saw took the shape that it did. For in the middle of the night I woke suddenly and sat up startled.

I found the room perfectly light; the door, which I had locked, flew open, and there walked in three ladies, dressed in the Queen Anne costume, with the pretty old stiff cardboard ornament of the head and everything. Never before had I understood how beautiful was the Queen Anne dress. The ladies sitting down on chairs round the fire (which was now burning merrily) began to talk, but I know not what they said. Suddenly - it shames me to confess the thing - I was seized with a horrid terror. I leaped from the bed, pulled back the curtain, and pulled up the blind. It was about three in the morning, and twilight. Then I turned to my visitors; they slowly faded away. The light slowly went out of the room; the fire slowly burned low; the figures slowly became faint; they slowly vanished. Who were they? Well. You see that I have seen things. But I have heard nothing. No communication has ever been made to me from the other world at all, except by the spirit Katie, and she only talked rubbish through a medium, and I had to pay a pound for it.

There will be much more about medums, the messages they conveyed and the psychic phenomena they manifested in a later chapter!

6
SOME FAMOUS PORTSMOUTH HAUNTINGS

GHOSTS OF WYMERING MANOR

If haunted houses can be celebrities, then Wymering Manor, at the foot of Portsdown Hill to the west of Cosham is most definitely a rock star.

The ancient manor house's history stretches back far into the distant past. The site is mentioned in the *Domesday Book* of 1086, its cellars (which still exist) are of Saxon origin, and

there is even archaeological evidence of Roman habitation of the site. It was once at the centre of a large estate stretching out over the Hampshire countryside down toward a lonely and desolate shoreline along which a solitary road stretched between Cosham and Fareham.

Its oldest documented owner was William Mauduit, who is recorded as marrying a Portchester woman called Hawyse in 1069. Mauduit owned other manors in Hampshire and was most likely one of the invading Normans of 1066.

The majority of Wymering Manor dates from the 16th Century, with a spacious wood-panelled hall dominated by two barley sugar twist balusters of the Elizabethan era. Reflecting the deep religious tensions of the times, the house even contains two priest holes.

In its later years the manor was bought by Portsmouth City Council to prevent it being demolished. The remaining garden was sold to developers (meaning it is now fenced in by a 20th Century housing estate) and it was then leased to the Youth Hostels Association. More lately, it fell into such disrepair that in 2013 it was sold by the council to the Wymering Manor Trust for one pound, along with a start-up grant to restore it.

You can imagine that with such a long history, the manor has collected numerous ghost stories - to such an extent that it was proclaimed by David Scanlan, founder of the Hampshire Ghost Society to be *Hampshire's Most Haunted House*.

A ROLL CALL OF WYMERING MANOR GHOSTS

The ghosts of the manor include:

THE LADY IN THE VIOLET DRESS

This apparition came to visit the joint owner of the house Thomas Knowlys-Parr in 1917. Thomas, reputed to be a direct descendant of Catherine Parr (the fortunate queen who survived King Henry VIII) owned the house with his aunt, Mrs Nightingale. One night he woke to find a figure dressed in blue at the foot of his bed. This Lady In Violet he recognised as the spirit of a cousin who had died in the same year. This was not a frightening encounter. She stood and chatted with Thomas for a while, seeming to want to spend a little time catching up, before adding:

"Well, Tommy dear, I must leave you now as we are waiting to receive Aunt Em."

At this point she vanished into thin air. The following morning Thomas received a telegram informing him that his Aunt Em had died during the night.

RECKLESS RODDY AND HIS PANICKED HORSE

The dastardly Sir Roderick of Portchester, local folklore tells us, lived during the Middle Ages. One night, the lecherous and wicked knight heard that a newly-wed bride had been left alone in the house while her husband was called away to deal with an emergency.

Filled with reckless and violent lust, Sir Roddy rode to the manor to rape the solitary bride.

Thankfully, her husband returned home and chased Sir Roderick out of the house, cutting him down with his sword as he attempted to make his escape on horseback. In panic, the horse bolted.

It is said that from time to time the ghostly sound of a panicked horses' hooves can still be heard clattering in the lane outside.

There have been various testimonies to the eerie sound of the ghost horse galloping away, including one during World War 2, and another from 1960, in which the Youth Hostel warden claimed to have heard it.

Though you might think he would have learned his lesson, the cruel Sir Roderick is said to appear if a newly-wed enters the house.

This legend may explain why Wymering Manor has no bridal - or bridle - suite!

THE GRISLY-HANDED NUN

This apparition has been seen on many occasions over the years. Stories abound of hearing a choir of nuns singing and chanting, a weird sound that presages the sighting of the spectre of the nun, who appears, hands dripping with blood, on the stairs to the attic. One local legend claims that the room above, known as Noah's Ark, is where the nuns performed abortions on members of their order who had formed illicit relationships with nearby monks. The bodies, it is claimed, were buried in the garden. To date, no infant's bones have been found there.

JANE AUSTEN'S BROTHER, SIR FRANCIS AUSTEN

Sir Francis was a naval officer who is buried at Wymering Church. This ghost does not appear to be particularly scary. One report says he "smiled at one of the staff".

Lord knows why he did that, but at least his hands weren't dripping with blood when he did it.

OTHER EFFECTS AND HAUNTED ROOMS

There are also reports of sudden drops in temperature, the spirits of whispering children, furniture moving - and a total of more than twenty apparitions. Perhaps as well as once being a Youth Hostel, Wymering Manor is also a ghost hostel. This would explain the constant spiritual traffic.

Haunted rooms are attractive features for any self-respecting ghost-hunter looking to stay a while and investigate. The Blue Room has a door that unlocks itself and stands open, while the Panelled Room is said to have a deeply oppressive air, as of a malevolent presence. People have been known to run from it shaking with fear. Indeed, the aforementioned hapless Youth Hostel warden is said to have been extremely uncomfortable in the room, and more so after he experienced feeling a hand on his shoulder, only to discover there was no-one else there.

LEGENDS OLD AND NEW

There is a story that smugglers' tunnels run from the manor to Wymering Church, and even to Southwick Priory - though once again, there is no evidence of this.

A new legend began thanks to a journalist in *The Daily Telegraph*, who wrote in an article that rather than chanting, the nuns were "scurrying" about. Anyone who knows anything about ghostly nuns knows they don't scurry, because that's not as scary, so not only was this a crime against tradition, but also against a damn good yarn.

The article in which this information appears is entitled *Council give away £375,000 manor 'because it is haunted.'*

Since that was not the reason it was given away, I detect some journalistic invention, especially because the source for this headline quote is not named...

Who knows? Perhaps the journalist was told about the supposed *real reason* for the transaction... by a ghost..!

PORTCHESTER CASTLE

With a history that stretches back to the Roman era, and further into the realm of myths and legends, we've already seen that Portchester Castle is a prime site to amass a residential spirit or two.

Its history is rich. In 1128 after a church was built inside the castle walls, the grounds became an Augustinian Priory. But in 1154, Henry II confiscated it, finding it useful as an embarkation point for France, as a treasury and as a prison. By the end of the Twelfth Century, it began to be superseded by the fortified town of Portsmouth, with its commanding position at the harbour entrance from which to defend the anchored fleet. Nevertheless, successive kings used the castle as an occasional palace, a hunting lodge or a garrison - and indeed in 1415 Henry V launched his invasion fleet from there, prior to his victory at the Battle of Agincourt.

Later still, after it had long fallen into disrepair, the castle was used by the Government during the Napoleonic Wars to house French prisoners of war. The conditions were brutal, with much violence and squalor.

Finally, by the middle of the 19th Century it had become a picturesque ruin. It was later given away, by the Thistlethwaite family which owns a large estate in this part of Hampshire, to English Heritage for preservation.

And so we have the wonderful recreational and historical tourist attraction that sits by the water today.

THE CRUSADER'S GHOST

Of course, without doubt, this ancient historic pile *must* be haunted. A fascinating report from the *Daily Herald* on 7th May 1928 sums up one ghostly presence. The article, simply titled *CASTLE GHOST*, tells how one well-known and oft-sighted spirit had been seen for the second time in close succession:

Portsmouth, Sunday - The ghost of the old warrior that is popularly supposed to haunt the beautiful ruins of ancient Portchester Castle has been seen again - at least so it is affirmed.

A party from Portsmouth was making a tour of the castle in the dusk, and one of the women went alone into a chamber of the keep. Later she rejoined the party, awesomely declaring that she had seen an apparition that looked like a warrior clad in armour.

Apparently the ghost was the one seen by a woman last October. She was strolling round the castle one dreary evening when there was a mist over the shores of Portsmouth Harbour on which the castle stands. Suddenly in the keep she saw a wraith-like figure resembling that of an old Crusader. He ascended some steps, passed into a chamber, and knelt down as though in prayer.

OTHER GHOSTLY INMATES

The crusader, however, isn't the only ghost said to haunt the castle. In 1930 the *Portsmouth Evening News* sent two intrepid journalists into the ruin to spend an adventurous spring night of investigations. Their 7th April article filled most of a page with their experiences, and descriptions of some of the other spirits associated with the site.

Among the spectres they listed were:

- a murdered warder with a spear
- the Castle custodian doomed to carry a stone upon his back until such time as he reaches the Priory at Southwick before dawn
- two French prisoners who fight an eternal dual with separated halves of scissors
- the wife of a German soldier, who drowned herself off the foreshore
- a gigantic ghostly boarhound.

The journalists really went to town on getting a spooky feel into their article. Regarding the soldier's wife who killed herself, they described walking along a route called "German Lane" in the night just before they entered the castle, and (very much playing for the goosebumps) described how a farm cart drawn up into a hedge looked "remarkably like a hearse"!

The reporters went on to say that some Portchester residents' relationships with the local ghosts had been terrifying. "So great, indeed, has been the impression made that there are cases on record where the person who has seen the unquiet spirit has moved from the haunted village on the earliest possible opportunity."

Once inside the castle, they described "the hole where the surgeons used to dissect the dead for experimental purposes", as well as the pit "where their prisoners were incarcerated" and a passage supported by buttresses "in the shape of erect coffins." All good Gothic stuff!

Their adventures in the night included getting bewilderingly lost in the castle complex by torchlight, unusual noises as of someone walking nearby, a terrible shriek from inside the castle, and the sound of something tap, tapping away - so they expected to see at any moment the "murdered warder appear, feeling his way with his spear butt."

All of these phenomena had their explanations. The sound of walking turned out to be a large rat, the terrible shriek was that of an owl and the tapping sound was the light rain they hadn't noticed outside dripping into a puddle.

The sightings that prompted this investigation, however, remain unexplained. Indeed, the *Western Daily Press* on 6th February 1930 reported that a new ghost had been seen at the castle:

ANOTHER CASTLE GHOST

SENTRY COMPANION TO THE CRUSADER WARRIOR
The ghostly Crusader, who is said to haunt Portchester Castle, Portsmouth, has been joined by another warrior spirit—a sentry. The castle is at present under restoration by the Office of Works and a tradesman who had delivered goods there declares that when leaving the grounds in his car in pitch darkness early in the morning he was terrified by the sight of a white human figure, standing into an angle of the Castle walls. The figure, he said, appeared be watching him. The new ghost is said to resemble a sentry. Some time ago a woman visitor to the Castle declared that, when crossing the keep to a breach in the West Wall which gives entrance to a spiral stairway, she was amazed to see the figure of a man dressed as a Crusader kneeling on the stairs.

Portchester Castle is a favourite place for ghost hunters. Understandably so, for it has many moods. On a summer evening, as the sun goes down, spreading sombre shadows across the grounds, darkness gathers at the feet of the walls and the stars come out over a fairy castle. On an autumn morning of thick sea fog, with foghorns lowing in the distance, the claustrophobic sense and lack of clarity can trick the eyes into seeing unclear movement in the mist. And on a winter's night, with a storm driving the waves ashore, the castle provides enough drama to stir even the most practical of souls to a sense of wonder.

PORTSMOUTH CATHEDRAL

One of the oldest buildings in Portsmouth itself is the old Church of St Thomas, which, in greatly extended form, became Portsmouth Cathedral.

The church takes its name from none other than the murdered Archbishop of Canterbury, St Thomas Beckett, who was butchered by knights loyal to King Henry II in Canterbury Cathedral in 1170.

The land for the original building's construction was gifted to the Church by the founder of Portsmouth, Sir Jean de Gisors, to build a chapel to Thomas, the "glorious Martyr". It was dedicated in 1188 and the original chapel is still identifiable at the eastern end of the Church.

In 1927, just before it was to be rededicated as a cathedral, a fascinating ghostly tale was told by the church's Archdeacon, soon to be its bishop, E. Neville Lovett, about the sighting of a historical ghost one winter evening. The *Portsmouth Evening News* of 25th January 1927 reported "an interesting story strongly suggestive of an apparition, is contained in a reverie which appears in the current issue of 'Portsmouth Parish Church Magazine' under the head of 'The Holy Blissful Martyr'."

The article reprints most of the story, which begins by describing how when one goes alone into an "ancient church, and waits motionless, it seldom happens that the silence seems unbroken. Every now and then, somewhere in the old building, there is a sound as of a footfall, a sense of someone moving, a feeling that one is not solitary, a creak as of a door opening, and sometimes, surely, a muttered word or two."

The narrator goes on to say that on December 29th, as he sat at the close of a short winter day, and the encroaching darkness "made the old building a confusion of shadows and gloom, the vague sense of some other human presence than my own took a definite form." He recounts how he was considering the life of St Thomas Beckett, and how his supposed descendant, Archdeacon Hardcastle of Canterbury Cathedral was his friend. Then the story takes an interesting turn, because now someone moves up the aisle to the chancel, silently and with no sound of walking. The writer realises that to be there, the figure must have come through the Sanctuary gates as if they were not there, because they were closed.

Now, the narrator peers through the gloom, but can see nothing clearly, only a deeper darkness that obscures the glimmering white altar, which is set for the Christmas festival. Fascinated, he moves toward the figure.

He describes what happens next:

As I did so, the kneeling figure was more clearly defined and when I had passed half-way along the chancel, I could see that he who knelt before the altar was a man of great stature and bulk. He wore what appeared to be a monk's habit, but it was all rent and torn, dirty and bloodstained. I noticed, however, that the sleeves were not the loose sleeves of the monastery, but close as if the habit was used to be worn beneath robes. One of the sleeves was all but rent away, and as the man knelt there with his back to me and his hands slightly raised and joined in prayer, even in the gloom I noticed the great biceps and thick hairy forearm, all bruised and gashed. The monkish and soiled habit, and that mighty though sorely damaged arm I saw; the head was only darkness from where I stood. I crept forward to the altar rails, I could not hold myself back.

Yet now I turned sick and faint, for the scalp and hair showed a horrible shapeless mass of coagulated blood and brains. Upon the crown of the skull had descended some terrible smashing blow. I sank upon my knees , partly from shock at the ghastly sight, and partly from a growing sense that I was in the presence of some awful happening of long ago, which had still some connection with this old building.

Then, I caught the sound of some prayer, said very soft and low in a voice deep and full of resonance. The words were not English, but Norman French, which I could fairly understand, and all the more easily because they have a very familiar English Form - 'Keep, we beseech Thee, O lord, Thy Church with Thy perpetual mercy: and because the frailty of man without Thee cannot but fall, keep us ever by Thy help from all things hurtful, and lead us to all things profitable to our salvation.'

Over and over again these words came in the pretty old Norman mother tongue; and soon I found myself whispering them after him, while my thoughts swayed backwards and forward, back to the long centuries of our old Church's story, a story so full of man's perpetual frailty, a story so full of God's perpetual mercy, and forward to the veiled future, when by God's grace the same old Church would take a useful part in leading us all more than ever, to things profitable for our salvation.

PRAYING TOGETHER

I ceased to wonder any more about that kneeling figure. I only knew that we were praying together as men do not often pray together, and that the past and the present and the future seemed to be merged in one. We kneeled thus for a long time. The church became quite dark. I could no longer see my companion, only I could still hear the low strong voice saying the same words, while each repetition seemed to draw me down more deeply into their significance.

The sound of a key turned in the vestry door on my right startled me. The verger was coming in to prepare the church for evensong. It is his manner, as he goes about his work, to sibilate softly to himself a hymn tune. This evening, I remember, I noticed it was 'The Saints of God their conflict past.' Entering, he turned left and switched on the Chancel lamps.

I instantly turned to where the stranger had been kneeling; I should see him clear now. But there was no-one and the sound of praying had ceased. I got up from my knees and turned to speak to the verger. He, too, had something to say to me, and he spoke first. 'I notice, Sir, that in entering that baptism in the register this morning, you put December 28; it's the 29th today.' 'Did I so! How stupid of me, of course December 29. Let me see: What happened on December 29? Why! It's the anniversary of the murder of St Thomas of Canterbury.'

It is an entertaining story from Archdeacon Lovett. However, what is interesting is that it came to the attention of the *Daily Express* who contacted him to ask about it. In interview, Lovett said:

"I wrote the story merely as an interesting experience. The friend who described it to me is quite reliable, but I related the story from a quite unbiased point of view."

The Archdeacon closed the interview with the remark:

"Who could the figure have been but the spirit of St Thomas, unless, of course, my friend had some kind of vision. No one can tell."

The story in the magazine later appeared in *Shadow Tales of Portsmouth Cathedral*, a collection of short stories drawn from a series published in the parish magazine. In the introduction, the author states that while the book contains elements of fact, the ghostly elements are pure fiction.

If this is true, then why did the Archdeacon of Portsmouth tell the large readership of the *Daily Express* that he had heard the story from a reliable friend, and that the ghost must have been St Thomas? Or, did he? Was he misreported?

This, perhaps is how legends begin.

Whatever the case, something doesn't add up...

...So, it's yet another... Mystery of Portsmouth!

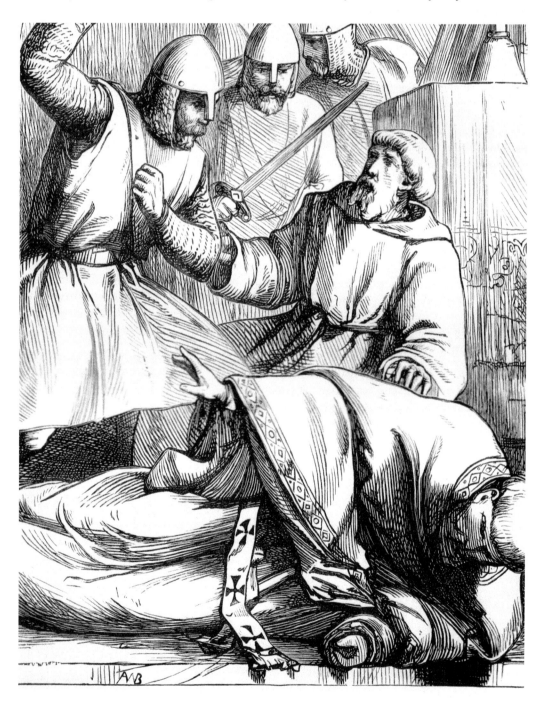

7
A FEW HOTEL AND PUB GHOSTS

TALES OF GHOSTS, BARS AND HOTELS

As a seaside resort visited by countless tourists, and also as the home of the Royal Navy, whose dockyard once employed tens of thousands of men, Portsmouth has its fair share of pubs, inns and hotels.

Many landlords in the Portsmouth area swear their pubs are haunted. For example, at The Fighting Cocks in Gosport, the landlady and two staff once told me they had seen glasses rise off the shelf and hurl themselves across the room. They added that there are also cold patches they say feel deeply eerie. Such stories aren't uncommon, though whether it's due to damp glasses sliding from shelves, drunkenness, or some other less tangible reason, who can say?

For a ghost to make its way from the bar-room into the newspapers, however, it often needs a backstory to stick in the public mind. In this short chapter I gather some Portsmouth-related tales from the papers, and show how ghost stories aren't always what they seem.

I then finish with a powerful account from the website www.british-paranormal.co.uk, which gives an eerie account of Portsmouth's Suicide Hotel.

AN UNCOMMON, EERIE TOWN

The uneasy haunted feeling people the world over sometimes experience is mentioned in a short article from the *Portsmouth Evening News* of 19th December, 1936. "In such an old town as Portsmouth," the writer tells us, "there are probably many houses in which strange noises may be heard caused by the wind behind the casements, the creaking of doors, or the contraction of the floor boards; but a very gallant officer once assured me that he would not sleep - or try to sleep again - in a certain house for a fortune. It was for him a night of terror, the loud and incessant noises resembling those of the main deck on a man-of-war in action."

The article, called *In the Dead of Night*, also tells how The Fountain Inn, Old Portsmouth had a reputation for being haunted, but tantalisingly gives no further detail.

The piece is in fact a taster for the annual set of Christmas ghost tales the newspaper printed in its supplement.

It sets the scene nicely for reports of haunted Portsmouth pubs and hotels.

FACT OR FICTION?

A detailed account of one Portsmouth apparition appeared in the *Hartlepool Northern Daily Mail* on 22nd December 1887. Described as a "Ghost story for yule tide", at first sight it appears to be one more Victorian Christmas Ghost Tale:

SLEEPING WITH A GHOST

A TERRIBLE NIGHT IN PORTSMOUTH

A strange occurrence happened to Mr. Hamilton, afterwards a well-known dockyard official at Portsmouth, about sixty years ago. Mr. Hamilton arrived one night in Portsmouth, a complete stranger, and as he was to leave for abroad next morning, strolled through the town to see where he could get put for the night. As ill luck would have it, the town was unusually full of strangers, and he could get his nose in nowhere. At last he came across a decent-looking public house up a quiet lane, where he inquired, and was informed that he might sleep in a double-bedded room, if he did not object to some other person occupying the other bed. But this he did object to, and after a little haggling he agreed to pay for both beds, and he soon retired to his room, carefully locking the door behind him to keep out intruders.

Well tired out with wandering about the streets, he undressed at once and slipped under the clothes.

He had slept perhaps an hour or more, when he was aroused by the noise of some carousing party in the lane below, and turning round in the bed, he suddenly perceived by the light of the moon shining brightly through the window that the other bed was occupied. A man, partially undressed, but having the appearance of a sailor, was half sitting, half lying, outside the clothes, having a Belcher handkerchief tied round his head by way of a nightcap.

At first Mr. Hamilton was indignant at this breach of faith on the part of the landlady, and he had serious thoughts of arousing the intruder and requesting him to leave the room; but seeing that the man was quiet, he at last determined to let matters rest as they were until morning.

It was broad daylight when he woke, and on looking across the room he saw that his strange fellow-occupant had never changed his posture, still remaining half reclined upon the quilt. His features were handsome, and he had a great black bushy beard, but the handkerchief round his head was white, although it was saturated in parts with a crimson fluid that trickled down his left cheek, and seemed to have run upon the pillow. Suspicious of foul play, Mr. Hamilton rose and went towards the door, which was still securely locked from the inside. He then approached the bed, one of the curtains, from his position, obscuring his view of the occupant. Reaching the bed, he was astonished to find that the man had disappeared. Scarcely an instant before he had seem him apparently sound asleep on the bed, and now he was nowhere to be seen. Mr. Hamilton at once examined the walls, and the flooring under the bed, to discover if any secret means of approach to the room might be gained; but despite a close scrutiny could find none.

Unable to rest more, he dressed and proceeded down stairs, where he endeavoured to extract some information from a servant girl, the first human being astir in the house, but could gain none. At last the landlady appeared, and when Mr. Hamilton began to reproach her with her breach of faith nothing could exceed her surprise. No one else had been shown into the room, she said, unless Mr. Hamilton had let someone in himself.

At length the guest passed out of the house, repeating as he went that there had been an intruder in the room, and that the intruder was possessed of a splendid pair of black whiskers. Glancing round for a moment, Mr. Hamilton was surprised to find that his last words had completely altered the appearance of the landlady. Her eyes were fixed, her cheek pale, her mouth half-open, and she stood like a statue. At last she said hurriedly,

"Come back, for Heaven's sake, and tell me who and what you saw in your bedroom last night."

Perceiving her agitation, Mr. Hamilton at once recounted the occurrence, dwelling minutely on the slightest particular, and describing as accurately as his memory would permit him the appearance of the sailor who had occupied the other bed

No sooner had he done so than the woman, lifting up her arms with every appearance of terror, cried out that she and her house were ruined forever. Mr. Hamilton was surprised beyond measure at this sudden outbreak, and he pressed for an explanation, and at last the landlady, exacting a promise from him of strict secrecy, told the following story:

On the third evening previous to that date a party of sailors bad been drinking in her house, and a quarrel arose between them and some marines from another ship. During the quarrel one of the sailors, a fine young fellow of five-and-twenty and corresponding exactly to the description given by Mr. Hamilton, was struck a heavy blow on the left temple with a pewter pot. He fell to the ground, and his companions at once carried him to the room that had been occupied by Mr. Hamilton, and laying him on the bed, endeavoured to staunch the blood. But their efforts we of no avail, and in a few minutes he died.

The landlady did not know what to do. She was in an agony of apprehension for the reputation of her house, and at last she consented to the body being buried in her garden, and that was done that very night by two of the murdered man's comrades. The man had been discharged, so they thought that no inquiry would be made after him.

"Now," the woman added, "he has come back to trouble us, for foul deeds will rise, and I never dare go into the room again."

So, was it just a ghost story for Christmas? And if so, why did it appear again in slightly different forms, below?

THE SAILOR'S SPIRIT RISES AGAIN... ...AND AGAIN!

An article from the *Portsmouth Evening News* dated 10th January 1934 echoes the tale told above, though it makes light of it. Not quite sure in which pub the story unfolded, the writer attributes it to the Old Blue Posts that used to stand on Broad Street, Old Portsmouth. Calling the ghost "Mr Whiskers", the story is very jolly and funny, and finishes by saying: "Now I hate to dismiss a ghost story in such a perfunctory manner, but if the wind and the draughts cannot open and shut a few of these doors in the typically mysterious way - thus conjuring up to the imagination a whole army of murdered seamen - then wind and draughts and doors are not what they used to be!"

Others, however, were far less lighthearted about the ghost. The *Dundee Evening Telegraph* reported on the 29th August 1936 that a Portsmouth resident took it extremely seriously.

TOMBSTONE FOR A "GHOST"

SAILOR WHO WAS MURDERED

A tombstone has just been erected at Portsmouth to the memory of a sailor who was murdered over 200 years ago. It is in a little courtyard which at one time was part of the Blue Posts coaching house, which flourished in Old Portsmouth for many years and which was burned down in 1870. Mrs S. Bowman, of Broad Street, Old Portsmouth, told a reporter the story of the murdered sailor which prompted her to place a tablet over the spot where his bones are supposed to lie.

One night early in the eighteenth entury a sailor carrying a heavy black bag entered the inn and took a room.

He warmed himself so liberally with rum that he foolishly told the company that his bag was full of money and jewels.

When he went to bed he was followed by a stranger who tried to snatch the bag. A fight took place, during which the stranger took out a knife and cut the sailor's throat.

When the landlady arrived, the stranger had gone and the sailor was lying dead.

The woman tied an old scarf round his neck and, with the help of her son, buried him in the yard.

Another traveller slept in the room where the crime had taken place a few nights later.

In the morning, the traveller asked the landlady why she had allowed another traveller to take a vacant bed in his room without notifying him.

"GHOST" IN BED

She assured him that he had been alone, but the man insisted, and described his room-mate as "a white-faced, ill-looking sailor, with a blood-red scarf round his neck."

The landlady, recognising the "ghost" of the murdered sailor, took fright and confessed.

Mrs Bowman has never seen the ghost, but she believes the story.

This version of the story is set a century earlier, and the murder is quite different. The following year another version of the tombstone tale was reported in the *Coventry Telegraph* and *Dundee Telegraph*, with the story now being described as "an ancient legend".

SHAPE-SHIFTING SPOOKY TALES

For me, one of the delights I find in such ghost stories is how they change over time. The story's details are incidentals, filled in as people see fit to make the events feel more real. In the first article, the story is told of someone in living memory. A handsome man with whiskers is buried in an unknown lodging in a quiet lane in Portsmouth. Fifty years later the story is considerably older, and the location is not a quiet lane, but Broad Street - once a bustling part of Old Portsmouth. The victim is either ugly or handsome. He is in a quarrel with marines who break his head with a tankard, or with an unknown assailant who cuts his throat. But in all cases, it's agreed he was buried in the garden, and his ghost haunts the bed where he died.

So we see that, just like their subjects, ghost stories can be elusive. Like mist or fog, they form into new shapes in the half light of memory and imagination...

42

INDIGNANT PRESSMEN

Another ghost story made the papers in *The Portsmouth Evening News* of 30th September 1881. What I enjoy about this one is the down-to-earth nature in which the writer dismisses it:

A PORTSMOUTH GHOST STORY

For the past few weeks the Sultan public-house, next door to the Prince's Theatre, Lake-road, has been closed, the tenant having left. On Wednesday, by some unexplained means, a story got wind that the place was haunted, and that a ghost was frequently to be seen at the windows. This was further circulated yesterday, with the result that hundreds of people came to see the spiritual visitor, and judging by what has occurred to-day, the crowd may reasonably be expected to be immensely increased tonight. One of the numerous tales afloat was to the effect that a man and woman, with their throats cut from ear to ear, were found in the cellar. There was, however, no foundation whatever for this and the other absurd stories, which have evidently been concocted by some imaginative or weak-minded individual.

The impatience of the journalist really shines through in this article. For him, people who believe in ghosts are "weak-minded" and the whole idea is absurd. And yet, the story made the newspapers anyway, and perhaps he forgot to consider that his own report might have helped swell those crowds he so badly criticised!

STICKLER FOR FACTS

The article above really goes alongside the next one, also from the *Portsmouth Evening News* from 2nd November 1901, in which an annoyed local reporter hits out at the nonsense written by a London journalist who was clearly trying to add a bit of mystery to a day that had gone badly wrong.

NELSON'S GHOST AND THE "GEORGE"

One of the special correspondents of the London morning papers who came down to report the arrival of *H.M.S. Ophir* at Portsmouth yesterday describes how he and some companions were left behind by the *Seagull* owing to the Press-boat leaving earlier than the hour specified on the original programme. "When the doughty Pressmen realised that they had been misled," says the writer, "they with one consent sought comfort at the 'George,' where the great Nelson slept his last sleep on earth, and where the superstitious say his ghost still rambles and reviles at the mismanagement of the Navy. The writer has slept at the 'George' many a time and thoroughly discredits the ghost story."

I can imagine the marooned London journalists getting drunk in the pub together, and trying to think up *something interesting* to file back at their papers in Fleet Street!

THE HAUNTING OF THE SKYLINE CLUB, NEW THEATRE ROYAL

The next ghost story is one of which I have personal knowledge.

That's not to say I ever encountered the ghost myself, but a good friend of mine who used to run an antiques shop on Albert Road, Southsea, thought he did.

He told me that in the 1960s he sometimes used to drink in the Skyline Club, which was located on the top floor of the New Theatre Royal, Guildhall Walk.

He continued, with a voice clearly perturbed by what he had experienced that there was most definitely a "strange, oppressive atmosphere" when you were there on your own late at night. Why he was there on his own he never said, but he remembered that one night he left the place terrified by some kind of presence.

So what was the story?

On 20th February 1958, a writer for the *West Sussex Gazette* gave us some detail about who the unquiet ghost might once have been, and in the way of the seasoned storyteller, sets up a punchline to take us back to the mundane world away from spirits:

GHOST WALKS AGAIN

I have made reference in this column on one or two occasions to the ghosts that are reputed to haunt the Theatre Royal, and I am assured that last week one of them was on the prowl again. It is believed to be the ghost of John Ruttley, who was actor-manager at the theatre from 1866-74, and shot himself in the dressing-room that now bears his name. All kinds of queer things are said to have taken place in the room since that time, and most people who have appeared at the theatre have refused to use it. One of those who had been most sceptical about the ghost was Mr. Robert Stigwood, an associate director of the company connected with the resident repertory company, but now he is not so sure.

One of the latest amenities at the theatre is the "Skyline" supper clubroom for members, where they can get a light meal after the show, dance until 1 a.m., and where young people can listen to rock 'n roll sessions.

Last week, when the "Skyline" had closed and customers left, two art students, who act as waiters in the clubroom, asked Mr. Stigwood to show them the haunted dressing-room. He and a friend, Mr. Shane Shaw, agreed to do so. While they were having a look over the rather bare looking room—it happened!

Mr. Stigwood said afterwards, "The lights suddenly went out and the door slammed. Then we heard angry footsteps up and down the corridor outside. We were rather scared, as there was no-one else in the building at the time, but when we looked out there was no-one to be seen. Naturally, we thought it was about time we went home, so we started to make our way out of the building and I turned the lights out in the corridor. But I had only gone about six yards when the lights clicked on again, although again there was no-one there. That really did it! I don't know what to believe now about the ghost."

Mr. Geoffrey Wren, general manager of the theatre, who heard the ghostly footsteps on another occasion, had an explanation about the "angry" quality of the footsteps.

"It may well be that Mr. Ruttley does not like being disturbed by these rock 'n' roll sessions," he remarked.

I must admit that Mr. Ruttley has my sympathies!

PSYCHIC RESIDUES

It is often said that ghosts are sighted at the scenes of awful murders, or mark places connected to extreme emotions - and that they are a kind of psychic residue of trauma.

The following story, which I have taken from the *British Paranormal* website was well investigated by writer A. L. Cuin. It tells a very dark tale.

This time there is no witty journalist to bring us out the other end of strange occurrences. I think this is a genuinely spine-tingling tale of ghostly happenings, and the story connected to it is a deeply melancholy one:

THE SUICIDE HOTEL, PORTSMOUTH

Cuin begins the account of this ghost story with a note that he has had to change the name of the hotel out of respect to the current owners.

The story starts with a place the writer dubs The Crown Hotel, which "was a medium-sized, early Victorian hotel," not far from the city's historic harbour.

The 170 year-old edifice was once a 15-bedroom building, had a bar, dining room and drawing room. After the war, it went into decline, and although it had once been quite grand, in its later years it targeted the lower end of the market, providing accommodation for travelling workers, benefits claimants, the homeless and so on - a common story for many seaside hotels, especially in the 1980s.

Yet even in its early days of grandeur, from close to the moment it opened, a "dark shadow" afflicted the building, he writes.

The hotel's first owner, a Mr Stroud of Southsea, was wealthy due to the family trade in importing rare animal skins and furs and he had a large portfolio of properties, at home and overseas. He was also a heartless and hard-hearted figure, who was reputed to be a deeply unpleasant employer who treated his employees cruelly.

The story goes that when he discovered that an unmarried 17-year-old chambermaid in his employ at the hotel was pregnant, he told her she could either give up the baby to a local orphanage, or she would be dismissed. Consequently, the mother, with no support from elsewhere, did indeed hand over the baby. This was clearly too much for her. She sank into depression, and six weeks later she was found dead in her room, having strangled herself with a tourniquet.

Cuin tells us that in 1954, more than a century later, new owners decided to expand the hotel by offering the three servants' rooms for hire along with the original 12 rooms.

Things soon went awry. Guests complained that room 15 was "oppressive" and "depressing", to such an extent that the owner feared for the hotel's reputation. This is why he closed it, reducing the number of rooms for hire to 14.

In 1986, the hotel changed hands again, being taken over by a large property management company during the "Costa Del Dole" period, in which in the absence of council houses the poor lodged in DHSS-paid rented rooms. The new owners renamed the hotel and renovated it, and, seeking to maximise their investment once more opened the abandoned room 15.

Cuin tells us: "The room was stripped and gutted. A small window was enlarged, allowing more light to enter the room. These changes seemed to precipitate a spell of paranormal activity that would culminate in the deaths of 3 people."

The first death that occurred was that of a young man from Spain, who took up residence in the newly renovated room while he worked at the nearby docks. He seemed to be a well-balanced and happy individual when he moved in, but "within weeks he had become withdrawn and deeply depressed."

After exactly six weeks from moving into the hotel, this formerly happy young man hanged himself in his room.

History repeated itself when the next occupant, a young woman, killed herself - once again, just six weeks after moving in. The pair of deaths was regarded by the management company as pure coincidence, and so the room was made available to let once more.

In 1988 an event occurred that changed the complexion of the case. Once again, a tenant committed suicide, and this time the young man left a suicide note describing how he had learned "how painful life was" since moving into the hotel.

Part of the letter, to the shock of those who knew the story of the room, made reference to "children being snatched from their parents" and of feeling like he had had his "heart cut out and thrown away".

This third suicide victim in just two years used a tourniquet to commit suicide. It was enough to spur the owners of the hotel into action, and the room was closed, never to be reopened for let. Today, the building is no longer a hotel, but has been turned into residential flats.

The investigator of this case does not give any details about the current fate of the room.

Was this all sad coincidence? A terrible series of unconnected tragedies? Did the awfulness of the suicides require *some sort of explanation*? Did people *need* the facts to be fitted into a certain shape to help them process it?

Whatever the case, you can read more from *British Paranormal* at their website www.british-paranormal.co.uk.

8
LESS RELIABLE PORTSMOUTH HAUNTINGS

Victoria Park Portsmouth.

THE VICTORIA PARK GHOST

It's fascinating to see how some accounts of ghosts change over time, or arise from a simple misunderstanding. Just so with our next ghost story. Depending on the mood of the journalist covering it, accounts of the sighting of the Victoria Park Ghost of 1912 are scary, exaggerated, add extra detail for effect - or are even quite silly.

A report of the ghost first appeared in the *Portsmouth Evening News* on Monday 19th August 1912.

Under the heading *A GHOST STORY*, it ran:

"Ghost-hunting" is the latest form of amusement with which Portsea folk pass their leisure moments. Nightly since Monday last week the novelty has been indulged in, and as the pastime now appears likely to interfere with public convention and to cause damage to public property, the offices of the police have been requisitioned. The Victoria Park has been the hunting ground, the Edinburgh Road entrance being surrounded each evening by a considerable crowd, which spent hours peering through the railing, endeavouring to catch a glimpse of the sleek, bony figure which is supposed to be dodging among the trees and monuments.

"Have you seen the ghost?" one asked the other with bated breath, pointing to a weird apparition a little way along the walk. Early in the week, some boys clambered over the railings to investigate the strange phenomenon and returned with stories of hair-raising thrills, which served to intensify the interest of the steadily growing crowds, who every now and then supposed they could see in the darkness the stealthy movement of the ghost, with long lean fingers that stretched towards them.

Mr Papworth, the head gardener, happened to be away on holidays. Mrs Papworth sent for the police. After a chase the boys were cleared from the grounds. Mrs Papworth also endeavoured to dispel the excitement of the crowd by explaining that the park was quite empty. But each evening there has been a repetition of the story. Children during the day have been heard to say "Are you going to see the ghost tonight?" On Sunday night, what up to then had been regarded as a stupid joke assumed a more serious aspect. A party of ten sailors scaled the gates and wandered round the park until a party of police appeared on the scene, when an exciting chase took place. The sailors rattled the back doors of the head gardener's lodge, made as much noise as possible with a tin they happened upon and generally raised the excitement of the crowd to a high state.

The origin of the story was an incident which occurred on Monday. A lady visitor to Mrs Papworth happened to be locked in the Park. Wild rumours of ghosts soon spread, and the superstitious beliefs of the crowd were deepened by the curious effect of the glare of an arc lamp upon one of the brass memorial plates. The movement of the intervening trees in the wind cast weird shadows over the place, which gave the idea to onlookers of a ghostly figure moving about.

This report was quickly picked up by newspapers up and down the country. *The Northampton Chronicle and Echo* of 21st August 1912 retold the story with a more playful tone, telling its readers in an article titled "GHOST CHASE AT PORTSMOUTH" that "excitement was caused at Victoria Park, Portsmouth, on Monday night by the report that a ghost was 'on the walk.'"

It went on to add (with the true journalists' creative eye) that "thousands" of people peered through the railings to get a glimpse of a mysterious visitant. It affirmed that many declared they had seen it "dancing weirdly about and waving its arms".

The dancing and the waving of arms is a new addition that fits the ghost into the common idea of the white sheet with eyeholes in it. *Any* self-respecting ghost must dance weirdly about and wave its arms!

For extra local colour, the report went on, "A posse of bluejackets and small boys scaled the railings to hunt for the 'ghost' and had to be chased by police. When ejected, they declared that they had seen the 'ghost' stalking about and had heard chains rattle."

This is a classic reworking of the facts for effect, mixing up the series of events of the boys climbing over the fence, with the sailors who went over it later. Told like this, it is a much more satisfying story, because it sounds as if it all happened in one night.

After reporting all the fuss and bother, the article gives a reason for the hullabaloo. "The prosaic explanation of the affair is that the steely rays of a street arc lamp were reflected on a large and highly polished name plate affixed to the obelisk commemorating those lost in the Victoria disaster, the effect of movement being imparted by the flickering shadow cast by trees swaying in the wind." The report finishes, "the clanking of chains was effected by an energetic bluejacket armed with a tin can and a stick."

This better-than-the-truth version was repeated in a shorter form the following day in the *Nottingham Journal*, which very much emphasised the "thousands" who had gathered to see it, and told how the police "repeatedly" had to clear boys from Victoria Park - when this happened only once in the original report. For extra detail a "chase over the flowerbeds" was added. This was then followed by the explanation of it all, thanks to the arc lamp.

By omitting the vital information that a person had been locked in the park, the *Nottingham Journal* was spinning the facts to tell a new story. It made the people of Portsmouth look a very superstitious bunch indeed and reveals a slightly ironic and mocking attitude.

This string of different reports on the same event shows one way Fake News was created in Edwardian England - through exaggeration, addition and omission.

By the time a journalist at the *Cambrian News* reported it on 30th August, the whole thing had turned in the direction it was always headed: farce. The report simply reads:

ANOTHER GHOST. Portsmouth is said to have a ghost that pays nightly visits to Victoria Park after the gates are closed. The ghost shakes its hands at the small boys who chase it over the flower beds. I do not like the idea of a ghost with hands, or that runs away from small boys.

What I like about this story is how it develops in just a few days.

Here we see how urban legends grow from very little indeed, in this case, a mistake with a park gate, a rumour and the civic benefit of electric lighting.

THE GHOST OF LADY TEMPLE

Another legend in a similar vein is that of Lady Temple's Lane. Going through Howell's *Topography of Portsmouth*, I encountered a note about a ghost story that was important enough to be included in a serious work on local history.

The entry described an area once called The Wilderness. This is now long gone. The Priory School at the top of Victoria Road North, Southsea, was built over it, as was part of Winston Churchill Road and the Fratton Road roundabout. The entry reads:

The Wilderness: A plot of land on the East side of Victoria Road North opposite Carlisle Road, on which part of the Higher Grade School now stands, was formerly so called. It was enclosed by a high wall and iron gates, and remained untouched and probably unentered, for many years. Rumour asserted that it was haunted by the

Ghost of Lady Temple, who is said to have poisoned her husband and then hanged herself from one of the trees in this plot.

It's a good story, and nearly makes it into my list of ghost stories and folk tales from Portsmouth. Sadly, however, the sober voice of fact gets in the way, as an article in the *Hampshire Telegraph* from the 1st March 1884 attests:

LADY TEMPLE'S LANE

The "Lady Temple's Lane," which until some fifteen years ago led in a semi-curved direction from the Fratton end of the thoroughfare now known as Victoria-road North, into Sommers-road, Southsea, obtained its name from a Lady Temple who once resided in a mansion standing on the site at present occupied by Chichester-terrace, Victoria-road. All kinds of rumours were current about the lady thirty years since, but the statements that she hung herself or committed suicide in some other dreadful way, that the mansion thereafter became haunted, and that her ghost might be seen walking at the rear of the mansion and in the neighbourhood of the lane, were of course a myth, with which juveniles were affrighted and adults amused. The lady in question was the wife of Sir Richard Godden Temple, and died a perfectly natural death. She was interred in the Kingston church-yard. The mansion which had been inhabited by the Temples was afterwards occupied by Mr Howard (the father of the late Town-Clerk of Portsmouth), and as Mayor he there had the honour of once entertaining William IV. The house was in later years removed. -C. T. G.

It's always a disappointment when a ghost story turns out to be unfounded. Whether children saw a tramp in the grounds after it fell into disuse many years later, or perhaps were frightened by a visitor late at night, who knows? But with its evocative name, The Wilderness is most definitely a contender for an excellent ghost story, should someone wish to resurrect Lady Temple, and write a new one! :)

STRANGE HEBREW APPARITION

Another fascinating mystery that is not quite what it seems was reported in the *Leeds Intelligencer* on 16th September 1854 and in the *Chester Chronicle* a week later. The story had the intriguing headline *GHOST IN PORTSMOUTH*, and reported the following bizarre phenomenon:

—During the last two nights (says the *Portsmouth Guardian*) the neighbourhood of the Jewish Synagogue has been for hours well nigh impassable. Crowds have collected despite the efforts of the police, in order to catch a glimpse of a ghost, which it is affirmed, disports its unearthly form in that locality. There is a rather remarkable dissimilarity in the descriptions of its appearance, for while some assert that it is like a gigantic Cochin China cock, with boots and spurs, and fifty tremendous horns, others maintain that it has glaring eyes, thirty-seven in number, and formidable hoofs, with a wideawake on its tail, and fire and brimstone issuing from its mouth. The apparition has created quite a sensation in the district.

Though the original story is supposedly in the *Portsmouth Guardian*, I have not been able to find it. Nevertheless, this strange story is full of its own mysteries.

Firstly, why, if such a stir was being made which involved the police controlling crowds in the streets, did no other newspaper in Portsmouth or Hampshire report it? I have made extensive searches, and so far have tracked down only this secondhand report.

Next, why is the apparition a gigantic Cochin China cock with boots and spurs, fifty tremendous horns, thirty-seven eyes, hoofs, a soft felt hat (ie: a wideawake) with fire and brimstone coming from its mouth? And, if it is such a horrific creature, who counted its thirty-seven eyes and fifty horns?

The fire and brimstone from its mouth might be the key to this mystery. It's a biblical expression used to denote God's wrath.

Is it possible, then, that this peculiar story presenting a demon with a soft felt hat - much like, for example, Fagin's hat in Oliver Twist - is inspired by Jewish stereotypes? Was it a piece of propaganda that came from the pen of someone with an axe to grind with the synagogue?

Who knows? But its fantastical elements and unsubstantiated claims that crowds made the road impassable looks like a fully concocted story. These days I suspect it would go very much in the category Fake News.

The only real mystery is why anyone should bother to make it up!

WRITING
ON WALL

Another synagogue ghost was reported in the *Daily Herald* on 9th August 1920, which turned out to be no mystery at all.

CROWD SEES GHOST
Mysterious Swaying Figure Seen Through Window Frame.

PORTSMOUTH Sunday.— A ghost rumour caused a large crowd to assemble at the rear of the Jewish Synagogue last night, where what appeared to be the swaying figure of a woman in white was plainly seen. A window was broken by excited sailors, but the ghost seemed unperturbed. To-day the apparition was found to be a length of wall-paper hanging from the ceiling.

BEDROOM
GHOST

A related ghost appeared five years later in the *Portsmouth Evening News* on the 5th October 1925. Described in the headline as a *Bedroom Ghost*, the article was dramatically subtitled *Uncanny Happenings at Southsea* and proclaimed that a "restless spirit" which had been seen flitting to and fro across a bedroom window, had "created uncanny excitement" in Southsea the preceding night.

The report went on:

The strange appearance was first noticed about 7 o'clock, and the story of a haunted bedroom rapidly passed from one person to another, until in the sultry evening atmosphere a large crowd of expectant

sightseers gathered. Soon 1,000 or more eyes were concentrated upon an open window in the second storey of an establishment which stands some distance from the roadway. There was no light in the room. All that could be seen was the dark aperture of the open window, and then there glided across a weird light, thin and vapoury, in the shape of the head and shoulders of a wraith. Again and again it crossed the window, irregular in appearance and restless in its manner.

The crowd in the roadway increased to such proportions that traffic was obstructed, and the only way in which the police could deal with the matter was for two of them to make a call at the house to lay the ghost by the heels. Developments were awaited for quite a long time, and at last the black "haunted" room was flooded with a blaze of electric light.

Satisfied that the apparition had been driven from its rendezvous, the crowd quickly dispersed.

One explanation of the phenomenon is that some juvenile occupants of the premises had manufactured the "ghost" with the aid of a sheet and an electric torch after retiring for the night.

SPIRIT
OF THE LAW

While the police intervened in the story above to apprehend the ghost, another report in the *Portsmouth Evening News* of 28th March 1932 described how supposed spiritual agency had intervened during a murder trial.

A PORTSMOUTH MURDER STORY Sir, —Re your article on our Cathedral Church, you refer to the burial place of Samuel Langley, who was done to death by one Jack Stacey.

With reference to Stacey, probably in the record of his trial you may find confirmation of a story I was told many years ago by an old Portmuthian that when under arrest, Stacey made some admissions or confessions. This was said to be due to the warder of the lock-up where he was confined wrapping himself in a sheet, visiting Stacey at night and appealing in a ghost like way to him, saying: "Stacey, Stacey, tell the truth." This led to further evidence and his ultimate conviction. The warder, I think, as a "reward", got sacked on the incident coming to light.

CLOSE SHAVE

Another ghostly Portsouth phenomenon, this time unexplained, was reported in the *Daily Mirror* on 1st December 1964. This report had an oddball feel to it that both amuses and leaves one wondering what the facts really were. The piece, entitled *The Ghost That Needs A Shave*, read:

THERE'S a ghost floating around who apparently needs a shave. For people living in a terrace house in St. Mary's-road, Portsmouth often hear the ghostly rattle of a shaving brush in a tin mug. Mr. Stephen Tiller, a 44-year-old clerk, says: "I have twice seen a white apparition on the stairs. It made my hair stand on end." His 23-year-old son, also named Stephen, said: "The spirit has never done us any real harm. In fact, we feel rather sorry for it."

And there the report ended. With this story I really enjoy the way the ghost's co-habitants had different reactions to it, with the son taking it all in his stride, while the dad was terrified. Perhaps ghosts aren't scary at all... until thinking about them makes them so.

PHANTOM
MENACE?

The following Portsmouth mystery was reported in the *Daily Herald* on 17th August 1953, headlined *The Grove Road Ghost Drove Car*:

A modern spook that could drive a car, was laid yesterday.

It first, appeared a fortnight ago when Mr. Gordon Banner, a Southsea organist, moved into a new house.

Every night he left his car - a Rolls Royce Phantom - at the top of the drive, facing the gate. On several mornings he found the car, still locked, 10 or 12 yards nearer the gate.

One night he heard a whirring noise, looked out and saw the car jerking forward, a few inches at a time.

On Saturday night he kept watch with a friend. Early yesterday the whirring started and the car jerked forward.

The two men crept up. On the front seat of the car was Mr. Banner's labrador dog fast asleep, but apparently having a nightmare.

As the dog's legs threshed about they touched the starter button and the car, which had been left in gear, jerked forward each time.

So, was it true? Would a man *really* not know he'd left his labrador on the front seat of his car? Would he not notice it the following morning? Would he not have the brains to put the evidence together? This one, looks very much like another case of Fake News!

So, why was it printed? - I hope this book shows that *news* is also *entertainment*, after all...

FANNY NELSON - NOW ON VIDEO!

Sometimes a story is better in the telling than in the evidence for it. With video, ghost sightings can be a disappointment. Just so with a "ghost" filmed on *HMS Victory*.

On 18th March 2018, an article appeared in the London newspaper, *Metro*, which described how a man working on *HMS Victory* claimed to see a ghost - and not just *any* ghost, but that of Fanny Nelson, wife of Admiral Lord Nelson.

The report, titled "Man thinks he filmed the ghost of Admiral Nelson's wife on the *HMS Victory*" [I am sorry to those who know that it is either "The *Victory*", or "*HMS Victory*", but never "*The HMS Victory*" - Ed] tells how Tony Ferguson, a personal trainer from Southampton with a deep interest in the paranormal happened upon the ghost while he was filming.

Ferguson explained that he had, since early childhood, seen ghosts, and very early on discovered that for some reason they gravitated toward him. He told how when he was a boy his grandad's house was haunted, and there was "loads of activity there with things flying around and the spirits of a man and girl always visiting so I was constantly surrounded by it." Ferguson claimed he realised he had a gift from a very young age, and that something in his energy attracts ghosts.

This is why, when he felt a pair of eyes upon him in the *Victory*, he knew a ghost must be nearby and so began filming. Ferguson claimed he didn't see it at the time, but on reviewing the footage, he could see the ghost plainly.

Yes, the footage does show a female figure in period dress moving on the deck, but there is nothing to substantiate his claim that it walked through a wall.

To see the footage for yourself, go to: https://metro.co.uk/2018/03/18/man-thinks-filmed-ghost-admiral-nelsons-wife-hms-victory-7397166

Anyone who has been in the Dockyard will know how notoriously difficult it is to distinguish ghosts from the numerous tour guides dressed in period costume...

What do you think?

PARANORMAL TV

Another paranormal event was captured on film and reported in the *Daily Mirror* of 28th July 2017 in one of the forts at the top of Portsdown Hill.

Fort Widley is often associated with ghosts. Built as part of the extended fortifications around Portsmouth in the 1860s when the older walls of the town around Old Portsmouth were removed, it has numerous tunnels beneath it, which some say are teeming with spiritual activity.

The *Daily Mirror* report is accompanied by video footage of the event. It shows a cameraman who suddenly moves forward as if he has been pushed, or as if he is moving away from something.

Filmed in darkness using low light cameras, the footage was taken while filming the tv show *Spirit Team*, and the report says the cameraman who was "shoved" is the one in the team who doesn't believe in ghosts. The film shows much confusion and swearing as the cameraman looks around for what pushed him. He appears baffled, develops the shakes, and finally uncovers his back to reveal it has light scratch marks on it. The cameraman was, we are told, so frightened he felt physically sick.

So, was this real contact? Or a nicely done publicity stunt for the *Spirit Team* tv show?

Have a look, here:

https://www.mirror.co.uk/news/weird-news/paranormal-cameraman-who-doesnt-believe-10888353

The great thing about video footage is you can decide for yourself!

9
A PECULIAR
COLLECTION OF
MYSTERIES

STRANGE & BIZARRE...

Now, to apparitions and inexplicable events, ranging from the bizarre, to the clearly exaggerated, to the utterly baffling, most of which made it into the newspapers. Prepare to encounter a gigantic ghostly rabbit, a spooked sentry, a mysterious humanoid - and a case of mass hysteria with the most tragic consequences.

In some cases the stories have explanations...

Some are clearly rumours that got out of hand...

...And there are also mysteries among these stories to be savoured and enjoyed!

CATCH THE WABBIT

In the film *Monty Python And The Holy Grail*, King Arthur and his band of knights confront The Killer Rabbit of Caerbannog in their quest for the Grail. At first dismissive of the animal, they soon discover it has a deeply vicious streak that leaves one of their party decapitated.

The fact is, Portsmouth beat the Python team to it by a century with its own sinister bunny: The White Rabbit of Portsea. This uncanny creature allegedly left people terrorised, and though it wasn't responsible for any decapitations, judging from the reports, the supernatural nature of the creature was indisputable.

A letter to the *Hampshire Telegraph* on 16th February 1884 describes the rabbit, which by then had already passed into urban legend:

THE "WHITE RABBIT" OF PORTSEA.

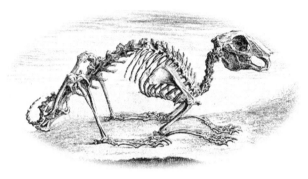

A correspondent signing himself "Old Inhabitant" writes: Having been born and bred in Portsea, I am in a position to answer to some extent the query of "G.W." respecting the "White Rabbit." So far as I could ever learn, the apparition - for such it was firmly believed by many to be - was the departed spirit of a man who "once upon a time" lived in the neighbourhood of the Buildings at the bottom of Frederick-street. Report had it that this man was very wicked, though wherein his wickedness consisted was apparently not quite clear. That he was very wicked, however, no one could doubt, for had not his spirit been condemned to haunt, in the form of a white rabbit, the neighbour-hood in which he had passed his lifetime? Many were the tales told of the appearances of this apparition, which was in the habit of coming and going in the conventional ghostly manner.

On one occasion, I have been informed, a soldier armed with his rifle, who was in the vicinity of the Buildings, saw the white rabbit suddenly start up from behind a stack of wood. With great presence of mind he raised his weapon and fired direct at the rabbit, which, instead of vanishing "into thin air," at once assumed colossal proportions. Greatly alarmed, the soldier fell to the ground, and on arising found that the rabbit had disappeared. Many were the attempts made by adventurous spirits to bring down the rabbit, which they regarded as nothing but a harmless live animal. I have been told that one man, armed with a gun, proceeded to the haunted spot with the object of killing the rabbit. The apparition obligingly made its appearance, but when its pursuer raised the gun to fire he was felled to the ground by some unseen force, and so shaken that he was obliged to keep to his bed for a fortnight.

Other tales, similar in their leading incidents to those I have given, have been, and still are, related by old inhabitants of the neighbourhood. All the freaks of the white rabbit appear to have taken place in the early part of the present century, and since its happy hunting ground has been taken in by the Dockyard Extension Works the apparition has, I believe, been seen no more.

I love this piece very much. How the story began and grew is baffling, but it's not the only large rabbit to have sinister connections. In the cult psychological thriller Donnie Darko, weird and inexplicable events revolve around a hallucinated 6 foot tall man in a rabbit suit. On a lighter note, Harvey, another six foot rabbit is the best pal of the eccentric Elwood P Dowd, played by James Stewart in the movie named after the creature, and then there's Wallace and Grommit in *The Curse of the Were-Rabbit*.

The White Rabbit of Portsea, then, is in illustrious company, and should perhaps have its own horror film. :)

SPRING-HEELED JACK

The phenomenon of Spring-Heeled Jack started in Victorian society with a few sightings in the 1830s and grew into a massive folk legend. At the height of the Spring-Heeled Jack scare, this inexplicable entity was reported up and down the country, with victims claiming him to be a super-athlete who spread terror wherever he went.

His exploits were dramatised in popular stories; plays about him were performed in cheap theatres nationwide. So deeply did he become engrained in the national psyche, he even became a character in some *Punch and Judy* shows. The title *Spring-Heeled Jack* became one of the nicknames for the Devil. Indeed, the Legend of the Devil's Footprints that began in Devon in 1855, in which a goat's hoofprints in the snow appeared to follow an impossible route, was also connected with Spring-Heeled Jack.

The fast spread of this amazing urban legend was perhaps in part caused by the easy availability of news in cheaply printed editions across the country. As we have already seen, a story reported in one part of the country was often repeated and exaggerated in another, while the meaning was changed or twisted as the reports took on a life of their own.

FIRST SIGHTING

The origins of Spring-Heeled, or Spring-Heel Jack are not entirely clear, but the first report of this strange creature is said to date back to London in 1837, when a servant girl called Mary Stevens was walking to work in Lavender Hill. At Clapham Common, a peculiar humanoid figure jumped out at her from a dark alley, immobilised her with a powerful grip, kissed her, tore at her clothes and grabbed her with its cold and clammy claws. Stevens' screams brought the aid of several local residents and the attacker fled at speed.

The following day, the creature jumped in front of a coach, causing it to crash and severely injure the coachman. Residents this time claimed he escaped by leaping over a 9-foot-high wall while babbling with high pitched laughter.

A WAGER OUT OF CONTROL?

Spring-Heeled Jack was officially recognised in 1838 when the Lord Mayor of London, Sir John Cowan, revealed in a public session that he had received an anonymous letter detailing a wager among unnamed members of the higher class that had led to various villages near London being terrorised by a miscreant dressed as, variously, a ghost, a bear and a devil.

Though Cowan was sceptical, a member of the audience confirmed "servant girls about Kensington, Hammersmith and Ealing tell dreadful stories of this ghost or devil."

From there, the story took on a life of its own. Numerous sightings around the country claimed the creature, ghost, or devil, could leap with superhuman ability, hence the nickname "Spring Heeled Jack". Sometimes it was claimed he had springs in the heels of his boots, at others that his leaping ability was wholly supernatural.

Jack had a specific look: a long dark cape, possibly with a white outfit beneath, a hideous appearance and metallic claws. Some claimed he breathed flame from his mouth. As the story took hold in the popular imagination, illustrations on the covers of penny dreadful magazines showed a figure somewhat reminiscent of DC Comics' Batman, who would arrive nearly a century later, and also had a deeply sinister aspect and extraordinary strength and agility.

SPRING-HEELED JACK IN POMPEY

As the folk-legend of Spring-Heeled Jack spread across the country, it was inevitable he would appear in Portsmouth. In his book *The Legend of Spring-heeled Jack*, Portsmouth University's Dr Karl Bell (an expert in the fabulously titled discipline of *Hauntology*) describes a sighting in the 1860s:

In his reminiscences about the town, F. J. Proctor recounted how 'a tremendous scare was caused by a dare-devil called "Springheel Jack", who had strong springs fixed to the soles of his boots and always popped up in uncanny places to the consternation of women and children'. He claimed to have watched Spring-heeled Jack's 'ghostly pantomime' as he leapt 'over tombs on a starry midnight', describing the figure as an 'ogre' dressed in white.

Proctor observed that 'like a rolling snowball pushed down a hill and gathering size', the tale of this apparition increased as it travelled, though 'ultimately it got too hot for "Springheel Jack", so he suddenly disappeared in the flesh'.

Dr Bell tells us F.J. Proctor recalled standing "awestruck among a crowd" watching the spook's leaps, though he also cautions that the account of one man writing many years after is not necessarily to be trusted. However, in the *Hampshire Telegraph* of 9th October 1878, there is separate confirmation of Spring-Heeled Jack's visit to Portsmouth:

The martial camp of Aldershot has again been honoured by a visit from that evil goblin known as 'Spring-heel Jack,' a celebrity, by the way, not altogether unknown to Portsmouth fame. Apparently, the audacious individual has gained courage from the seeming inability of the military authorities to summarily terminate his mischievous pranks, and his little pleasantries of last year are being repeated with increased hardihood for the amusement of sentries on isolated posts. Whether the courageous being is the same Spring-heel Jack as on previous occasions, we cannot pretend to say, but his nocturnal wanderings are pursued pretty much under the same circumstances, and attended by precisely the same results. He has been fired upon more than once, we are informed, but, as would become an orthodox ghost, has always escaped scatheless, while, to make matters still more wonderful, civil and military police have tried night after night in vain to capture him.

It is thus possible to tentatively date Spring-Heeled Jack's visit to Portsmouth to the preceding year of 1877, since the writer refers to his "little pleasantries of last year", though admittedly he doesn't specify if these pleasantries were confined to Aldershot alone, or Portsmouth.

A FRUSTRATING FELLOW

The writer was clearly unimpressed by Jack's Aldershot antics:

"Seriously speaking, however, it is scarcely creditable that such idiotic tricks remain unexposed," he wrote. "Practical jokes may be tolerated to a certain extent, but to suddenly pounce upon people in out-of-the-way places at night and frighten them within an inch of their lives by a wonderful display of agility is a feat no one short of a Bedlamite would think of performing... Should he, however, by some untoward chance fall into the kindly clutches of his friends, we may expect him to be brought to a tribunal which will deal for punishment with little regard to his supernatural attributes. Even the prosaic treadmill may be suggested as a mild corrective to ghostly visitations."

Despite the writer's wish he would desist, the legend of Spring-Heeled Jack lingered on into the 20th Century, with the last sighting coming as late as 1904. By this time, however, Jack had become what F J Proctor describes as a ghost in "a bedtime story in many an inglenook of Old Portsmouth".

What Jack was, and how he came to be, remains a mystery, but Portsmouth undoubtedly has its role to play in the legend!

THE GHOST AND THE SENTRY

If Spring-Heeled Jack really were an ordinary man, then jumping out at sentries would seem to be a rash business, especially considering the story reported in the *Portsmouth Evening News* on 24th January 1899. It begins:

SENTRY FIRES ON THE GUARD EXTRAORDINARY AFFAIR AT FORTON.

A most mysterious and sensational affair occurred early this morning at the R.M.L.I. Barracks at Forton, and as a result of the inexplicable action of a sentry, a lance-corporal of the corps is now lying seriously wounded.

The report describes how at two o'clock in the morning a group of Royal Marines approached the sentry box near the Pay Office Post in Forton Barracks, Gosport, to relieve the sentry, Private Henry Sutton. As they approached, rather than meet them with the challenge: "Who goes there?" Sutton raised his Lee-Metford rifle and fired.

Three of the men threw themselves on the ground for cover, but their leader, Lance-Corporal Davis, called out, "Stow that, you fool. Don't you see we are the relief?" Sutton fired three more shots. The first grazed the side of Davis's head, the second passed through his thigh. Civilians on the far side of the Barracks wall were also nearly hit.

With Davis down, his three colleagues fixed bayonets and charged Sutton, whom they disarmed and detained.

Davis was taken to Haslar Hospital, where he lay injured, while Sutton was held in the Barracks jail, awaiting civil police arrest.

Private Sutton's behaviour was a mystery. Standing orders strictly forbade the loading of rifles on sentry duty. Bullets were supplied, but with instructions they were only to be loaded at an officer's command. Sutton remained completely silent, unwilling or unable to give any account for his actions. Later, when asked by a commanding officer why he shot, he replied that he didn't know.

Here was a conundrum for the local press to unravel. In a long and rambling article written on the morning after the incident, the local reporter decided to fill in the gaps in information with speculation. He suggested there were only three reasons why Private Sutton fired: because he was mad, because he had a grudge against Davis, or because he had been frightened by ghost stories.

While there was no definitive evidence one way or the other as to his sanity, the journalist pointed out that Sutton was newly arrived from the Royal Marines Depot at Deal, and thus could surely not have built so strong a grudge against Davis in so short a time. This left the theory that Sutton was frightened by tales of spirits.

The journalist went on to explain that it was a habit of old hands at the Barracks to tell frightening stories to new arrivals, and that there had been some strange events, possibly pranks, associated with the area:

THE HAUNTED POST

As to the possibility that the young fellow discharged his rifle while in a state of acute alarm, it is well known that some superstitious people have given a bad name to certain parts of the barrack-ground, alleging that these particular spots are haunted. But a few weeks age a sentry at this very Pay Office Post was suddenly alarmed by having a lantern flashed upon him from the other side-of the high wall, a voice afterward inquiring the way to the magazine. Again, some months ago, a sentry stationed in the vicinity of the magazine alleged that he was attacked in the night by a black man, at whom he fired without effect. At all events, whether the story of the black man was true or false this sentry was found to be suffering from an injured finger, the wound being serious enough to warrant his discharge from the Service.

This paragraph, out of the whole 1600 word article was to be the one that caught the imagination of the editors of provincial newspapers up and down the country. Soon the story of *The Haunted Sentry Post* was being repeated and magnified in newspaper rooms looking for the latest sensation to fill their column-inches. The report appeared over and over, growing in clarity and focus until the story was retailed with certainty that stories of ghosts - and fear of hauntings - were the cause of the shooting.

So it was that the *Taunton Courier, and Western Advertiser* on 1st February 1899 ran the following headline and article, which embellished the affair with a little more information:

"GHOSTS" AT FORTON BARRACKS. FRIGHTENED SENTRY SHOOTS CORPORAL.

An extraordinary affair took place in the early hours of Tuesday morning at Forton Barracks, the headquarters of the Portsmouth division of the Royal Marine Light Infantry, a non-commissioned officer being shot by a sentry as the result, it is thought, of sheer fright.

Forton has the reputation for being a most fruitful provider of sensations. Close by is a burying place, wherein lie the bodies of hundreds of French prisoners, whose ghosts are said to perambulate the vicinity every now and again. It was this belief, it may be remembered, which led to mishap to a sentry a few months ago.

Early on Tuesday morning Private Sutton provided yet another sensation. At two o'clock Lance-Corporal A. V. Davis, with four privates, were relieving guard, and when they approached the Pay Office, where Sutton was on guard, the latter suddenly presented his rifle and fired four shots in rapid succession. Two of the bullets took effect on Davis, one grazing his head and taking off some of his hair, and the other penetrating one of his thighs, but fortunately missing the bone and arteries.

On hearing the reports, the guards charged Sutton with fixed bayonets, and made him a prisoner. The sentry quietly submitted. He made no statement, and has refused to give any account as to what induced him. He is a young recruit, and this was the first time of his doing sentry-go. Luckily his marksmanship is not of high order. Otherwise his four shots would probably have resulted in four funerals.

It is believed that some of the older men had been amusing themselves by telling him tales of that particular place being haunted, with a view of frightening him, and that on hearing the advancing footsteps he fired the shots out of funk. Davis was one of the Marines who took part in the Benin expedition. Though badly hurt, his condition is not at all critical.

There was no evidence that Davis had been told ghost stories by men at the barracks - this had merely been a suggestion of the *Portsmouth Evening News* journalist trying to weigh up all the possibilities - yet by the time it was reported in the *Taunton Courier and Western Advertiser*, this was given as the sole reason for the shooting, while information that Davis was detained for mental observation was ignored.

It is fascinating to think that in the modern day, the distortion, deletion and addition that occurred over a week in the Victorian era now happens in seconds on social media. There is quite a lesson to be had from watching this slower-paced spread of rumour. It is far easier to track!

A WILDCAT AT HAYLING

Talking of tracking things, we come to legends of large wild animals in the UK. Folk tales of the Black Dog as a harbinger of doom or as an emissary of hell go back centuries, and even inspired Sir Arthur Conan Doyle's *Hound of the Baskervilles*. But in the later part of the 20th Century, such sightings began to be accompanied by reported sightings of big cats.

This was the case with the Surrey Puma - a mysterious larger-than-normal cat sighted on the Hampshire and Surrey border from 1963 onwards.

As is often the case, many commentators dismissed these sightings as the results of over-active imaginations. But then a paw print was found and a plaster cast made. The paw was measured at around 12cm wide and was identified by London Zoo as that of a very large puma.

The cat was so big *and* real it had in fact lacerated a bullock.

Sightings of the puma continued, with 362 reports in total from the mid-1960s. There was an inconclusive photograph taken of the elusive beast, but the possibility of a real puma in Hampshire fired the public imagination, and

other sightings occurred throughout the country over the following decades.

The more famous ones included The Beast of Bodmin Moor and the Peak District Panther. All these were elusive creatures on the edge of rumour that inspired unproven theories about what they really were. Then, in 1975, a black panther cub was captured at East Peckham, Kent, and it began to look as if some of these sightings across the country might be true.

This was also the case with the Hayling Island big cat, which obliged cryptozoologists in their enquiries by being run down by a car in 1988. So, with a careless step, the Beast of Hayling Island emerged from myth into the full glare of national publicity.

Investigations showed it was an African swamp cat, more at home in Lower Egypt, the Middle East and Asia than a seaside resort on the south coast of England. How it got there remains a mystery, but anyone wishing to see it should make enquiries with Hampshire museums. It is now stuffed and mounted in a glass case and is often displayed at the Havant Museum, or is held by the Hampshire County Arts and Museum Service at Winchester.

Though it was the end of the road for this cat (excuse the pun), which was affectionately nicknamed *Swampy* by the museum staff, it was not the end of the Hayling Island big cat story.

On 31st March 2005, the Portsmouth *News* reported that Hayling Islander Andrew White had caught sight of another wildcat. He glimpsed the animal while driving along the northern part of West Lane on March 15th 2005, describing it as a "black, panther-like cat, with a very long tail." It was big enough to leap effortlessly over a six-foot hedge, the article added.

So, did the swamp cat mate with a domestic cat on Hayling Island and produce offspring? - Or is there a small family of swamp cats - or even panthers - loose on the island, even to this day?

One more mystery to answer!

A GHOSTLY THIEF?

Sometimes it is hard to imagine that much of the island of Portsea was once countryside and farmland, interspersed with villages. The Green Lane mentioned in the next article is in fact the modernday Somers Road, which at the time was already a built-up area, though not far from open countryside. It is the setting for the next account of a Portsmouth ghost that was not what it seemed. It led to tragic consequences which the perpetrators surely could not have imagined. This account, from the *Berkshire Chronicle* of 19th March 1825, speaks for itself:

GHOSTS NEAR PORTSMOUTH

—A curious attempt at robbery took place a short time since, near this town. A gentleman, who was returning home after spending the evening at a friend's house, a short distance in the country, when crossing a field (the night being dark) saw something approach him which appeared very tall, and concluding it was the ghost with which the neighbourhood had, for some time past, been represented to be infested, was resolved to see what it was.

When the ghost advanced near to him it threw open what he supposed to be a cloak, and discovered an appearance intended to represent a skeleton with glaring eyes. The gentleman then drew back slowly, and the ghost was advancing, when he heard a noise on his right, and a man suddenly appeared, who demanded to know where he was going, and on his asking what business that was of his, the man drew from his bosom a pistol, and with oath demanded his money. The gentleman having with him stout stick, struck the hand of the fellow, and the pistol went off. He then gave him a back-handed blow with the stick and knocked him down; and seeing the ghost, who had altered his appearance, preparing to attack him, made his escape; and having procured assistance returned to the the spot, but unfortunately could not find the delinquents.

This is the only attempt at highway robbery that has been heard of in this neighbourhood for some years past. This story being in circulation, tempted two idle young men to the mad frolic of trying to frighten their neighbours, and having suddenly made their appearance in Green-lane, one mounted on the shoulders of the other, with a white sheet covering both, the apparently tall and supernatural figure caught the attention of several persons at that time (about ten o'clock in the evening) gossiping near their homes, when one of them exclaimed, "here's the ghost coming."

The terror, in consequence, became general; and lamentable to relate, was fatal to a young woman who was far advanced in a state of pregnancy, and whose husband has just gone to sea; for, having escaped into her house, she sunk down in the fright, and in less than twenty-four hours had ceased to exist.

The delinquents are known, but hitherto they have escaped the vigilance of the peace officers, who are in pursuit of them.

BEWARE THE FIELDS AND WOODS IN THE NIGHT

It is often said that stories of ghosts in the wilder parts of the countryside were encouraged by smugglers to ensure that people were too frightened to go abroad while they plied their trade.

That highwaymen and robbers were also part of the mix shows that there were, in fact, quite solid reasons to avoid the quiet places of the countryside after dark - let alone ethereal reasons!

10

FORTUNE-TELLING AND WITCHCRAFT

A PLAGUE OF FORTUNE-TELLERS

One great mystery we all face is what our future holds for us. Our desire to be one step ahead of fate has spawned countless ways to see into the future, with palmistry, crystal-gazing and astrology among many other forms of divination.

Could these practices be real? The law certainly used to be clear on the matter! The 1824 Vagrancy Act made "any person pretending or professing to tell fortunes, or using any subtle craft, means or device, by palmistry or otherwise, to deceive and impose upon any person" liable to a maximum of three months' imprisonment. But the Act sat uncomfortably in a seaside town like Portsmouth, where holiday-goers sought entertainment from crystal-gazers and palmists, and the tradition of fortune-telling on piers was largely seen as harmless fun.

There were, however, some extremely unscrupulous operators who knew just how to press the right buttons of gullible clients - and the authorities sought to stamp out fortune-telling through the courts. Reports show how persuasive some such practitioners were, and how easy it is to manipulate a person's need for mysteries to be answered!

NICE LITTLE EARNER?

In the *Portsmouth Evening News* of 4th November 1886, a court report tells the case of Rose Smith, described as a "hawker with child in her arms", charged with pretending to tell the fortune of Emmeline Treagust, a general servant at Braemar House, St. Andrews Road, Southsea.

The story is a classic account of how travelling fortune-tellers worked house-to-house, promising news of future loves, of great fortune ahead, and offering to make an astrological chart, known as "ruling, drawing or predicting the planet".

The court found the whole affair ridiculous, frequently bursting into laughter. Even the account of Rose Smith's arrival at Braemar House offering to sell Treagust lace, and then offering to tell her fortune, caused much hilarity:

—Mr. H. Fisk (Assistant Clerk): And did you consent?
— Emmeline Treagust (Witness): Yes.
—What did she tell you? (Laughter.)
—She said that I had a fair young man, that he was abroad, that he was coming home, and that I should be married before I was twenty. (Renewed laughter.)
— And, if it's a fair question, how old are you now?
—I am nineteen years old now.
—And have you got a fair young man abroad (Roars of laughter.)
—Witness replied in the negative, and continued by saying that the prisoner asked her for the largest piece of silver she had, and that she would predict the "planet" on the day following. (Laughter.)
— What did you think that was?
—I thought it would be a piece of paper. She said she would bring the money back in the morning. (Great laughter.)
— Did you believe that?
—Witness, however, only laughed, but said that the prisoner asked her to lend her a pocket handkerchief to tie the money up in.
—And did you lend her a handkerchief?
—Witness said she did.
—What money did you tie up?
—A half-crown. (Laughter.) She first charged me sixpence to tell my fortune, and then said that she wanted the half-crown to rule the "planet." (Roars of laughter.)

In the case so far, Smith had got the equivalent of £15 in modern money from the hapless Treagust, along with a handkerchief.

The case continued, describing how Smith then read the fortune of Frances Stephens, a nurse at Braemar House, who gave her sixpence. Stephens's account was a similar story to that of Treagust, as she told the court, to much laughter:

"She told me that I hadn't been here long, that my young man was not far from here (renewed laughter), that he was a very dark young man, and that I should be married before I was twenty-one. (Great laughter.) She also said that I should spend a happy Christmas and not like I had last Christmas.

"She then asked me how much money I had, and I told her I had not got much; but she asked me to put the largest piece of silver I had into her hand, and said that she would bring it back the next day."

This promise of returning the money caused even more laughter!

Stephens's account wasn't finished there, however, and she went on:

"I told her that the largest piece of silver I had was a two-shilling piece, and she then told me that the last witness had given her a half crown. I put a two shilling piece into her hand, and she said that I was to wish four times."

The Assistant Clerk then asked: "Did you wish four times?" In the face of roars of laughter, poor Frances Stephens kept an embarrassed silence, but she went on to explain that the prisoner, Rose Smith, told her she was bound to have the two-shilling piece to rule the "planet" with, and added that "as the other witness had given her a half-crown it would be 'even money' if she gave her another sixpence". It was a raucous court-room that day, with more laughter at each answer Stephens gave.

Just so, when the Assistant-Clerk of the court asked what she thought the "planet" was and Stephens replied simply, "A piece of paper".

When Frances Stephens told the court that she gave Smith the money for telling her fortune, "but she said she would bring the money back," the room was uncontrollable.

In her brief talks with Treagust and Stephens, Smith took six shillings from them, which is around £30 in today's money.

Not long after this, she returned to the house and explained that the money Treagust had given her was not sufficient to rule her planet.

By this time Treagust was clearly suspicious. In the court case it was suggested Smith had been doing the rounds of young women in the area who were worried about marriage, and in each case spun them all a similar story.

For her troubles, Smith was imprisoned for 14 days.

LITTLE GOLDMINE

A similar story was reported in the *Hampshire Telegraph* on 28th May 1887. This time the court heard with some disbelief how much the defendant managed to take from Elizabeth Merchant, a domestic servant employed by Mr Bridge of Sussex Lodge, Sussex Road, Southsea. The defendant was Eliza Lowe, alias Stanley, 20, who appeared in the dock with an infant in her arms. The report in part reads:

FORTUNE TELLING EXTRAORDINARY AT SOUTHSEA

Elizabeth Merchant... stated that the prisoner came to her at the address named, and wanted to tell the fortunes of herself and a fellow servant. Prisoner told witness that she was to leave her situation, and that someone was to take her place.

— The Clerk: What was to become of you?
— Witness: I don't know. (Laughter.) She said I was to receive a lot of money, and that she generally charged sixpence for telling fortunes.

Elizabeth Merchant said she told Eliza Lowe that she didn't have sixpence, but conceded that she did have threepence, which she gave her.

This was a mistake. About ten days later, Eliza Lowe returned, this time offering to "rule her planet." Lowe insisted on a fixed amount of money, a half crown - around £15 in today's money.

When the witness replied that she had nothing but gold, the prisoner told her to tie a half-sovereign (equivalent to about £60) in the corner of a handkerchief, telling her "she only wanted it for a week."

Merchant did as she was bid, and gave her the money in a handkerchief. Unsurprisingly, Lowe later came back to the house again saying she wanted more.

When Merchant told her she had none to give, the fortune-teller explained, "What you have given me is not heavy enough to draw your planet off."

(This once again caused the court to erupt in laughter.)

Lowe would not be deterred, and then asked Merchant if she had any jewellery?

Elizabeth Merchant replied that she had two gold rings and a pair of earrings, which, at the direction of the accused, she tied in a high quality black silk handkerchief, which was all the poor girl had.

Lowe replied that it would do and promised to return the money and all the articles she had taken from the servant girl the following Monday.

Predictably, this wasn't the end of the story. The following Saturday, Lowe came to her again and this time asked for her watch, repeating that what she had already obtained was "not heavy enough to draw it off, as she would like to have it drawn off."

Elizabeth Merchant placed her watch in an envelope, sealed it and handed it to the prisoner, who once again promised to return all the articles on the following Monday at "either half past one or five in the evening."

When the following Monday came, Eliza Lowe did indeed return to see Elizabeth Merchant. She did not bring back her possessions, as promised, but instead demanded that Merchant give her her month's wages, once again saying that all she had was 'not sufficient to "draw it off".

In some puzzlement in the court, the Clerk asked:
"Draw what off?"

To which Merchant replied a little bewildered and to much laughter:
"The planet I suppose."

Eliza Lowe clearly knew she was on to a good thing. She returned again and this time received a half sovereign from another servant, Louisa Rapson, who tied it in a handkerchief just as Merchant had done. In return, Lowe told Rapson that she would receive a letter and photographs, which were related to her hopes for getting married.

The report continues:

On the next Saturday prisoner came again, and Rapson tied a sovereign and a gold ring into another handkerchief. Prisoner asked for Rapson's watch, but she replied she had not one.

Altogether Rapson parted with 30s and two gold rings, and Merchant handed over half a sovereign, two rings and a pair of gold earrings.

In today's money, the 40 shillings Lowe received is equivalent to around £250!

This still wasn't the end of the matter.

Once again, Lowe returned, and this time demanded both Rapson's and Merchant's month's wages. Rapson told her they hadn't received their wages yet, although they were due.

BLOOD
BOOK

The hearing continued with the testimony of another domestic servant, Margaret Conway of Surrey Cottage, Yarborough Road, Southsea. From her, Lowe took a sixpence, for which she told her that she "had a very hard life, and the future would be better," and that Conway would "find her difficulties between then and next August". She also told her that there was a dark man near at hand after her, and that she should "have a letter in a day or two which would have more in it than the other." (Laughter.)

In seeking to draw more money from Conway, Lowe promised she could "rule her planet" and make her life better, turning her fortune and bringing her luck. When Conway seemed reluctant, Lowe tried a new tactic, challenging her to be brave:

"You are not afraid?"

She then went on to talk about the changes of the moon and stars, telling Conway she only had to look in Lowe's "blood book" for more knowledge.

She asked Conway if she had ever heard of that book, and when she said she hadn't, went on, "It is a great big book, as big as this white stone (pointing to the doorstep), and if you came with me you would see all the jewels and money in my blood book."

Lowe claimed a local doctor and his servants had given her £20 a few days before - £2,500 in today's money. The Clerk asked if this was for telling his fortune, and when Conway replied "Yes, sir," the court burst into laughter again.

"YOU WON'T
DECEIVE ME?"

Next, Lowe told Conway to place all her money in a stocking, put it in Lowe's palm and "wish the day." Lowe said of the amount she needed:

"The more you have got the better." Conway told the court how she'd naively asked "is it?" Amidst roars of laughter she told how she then gave the money to the prisoner.

With a pang of uncertainty, the servant girl then asked:

"You won't deceive me?"

Lowe replied, "No, my darling." She told her that she lived at 210, Queen-street, Portsea, and that her name was Mrs. Lowe, adding that if she went to that address on the following day she would return the money.

The next day, Conway went to Queen-street as instructed. Unsurprisingly she could find no number 210. Then, when she saw Lowe again, she asked her when she was going to bring her money back. Lowe replied: "At twenty past four, if I can get it back from the person I lent it to."

This last charge the prisoner denied, but Conway was insistent that it was true and that she was positive as to Lowe's identity. The Clerk of the Court, Mr Feltham then asked:

— Have you ever had your fortune told before?
— Witness: No; this was the first time I had ever had it done.
— The Clerk : Let it be the last.
— Witness: I will take care that it is. (Laughter.)

The *Hampshire Telegraph* reported Lowe's home to be "a gipsys' van in Speck's Lane, Fratton," an address that fitted well with Victorian distrust of Romanies.

From these few witnesses, the equivalent of hundreds of pounds was taken by Lowe, who was clearly a smooth operator. The report finished with a statement from the defence, which tried to shift the blame to the witnesses:

One of the most extraordinary features in the case was the credulity of the witnesses, which was almost passing understanding, and he thought the Magistrates would agree that of whatever the prisoner had been guilty the witnesses for the prosecution had to a certain extent participated in by so foolishly and recklessly parting with their money, believing that they were going to get a return for it.

This argument, however, was rejected by the magistrates:

— Alderman Kent said the Act of Parliament under which the prisoner was charged was passed to protect young women like the witnesses from the intrigues of women like the prisoner, and Lowe was sentenced to three months hard labour.

TECHNIQUES OF FORTUNE-TELLERS

Newspaper reports of the time reveal how techniques used by fortune-tellers included offering to give information about rivals in love, how long clients would live, news of when they would marry, or "drawing the planet" for good luck, by creating a chart. The case of Alice Stanley, alias Kate Smith, who asked servant girl Florence Louise Martin to take money from the till of her employer on Fawcett Road reveals how fortune-tellers played on people's insecurities.

To get her attention, the report tells how Smith said:

"Your young man is tall and dark."

This immediately grabbed Martin's attention, and she asked her how she knew. Kate Smith capitalised on the opening and added:

"There is a girl with dark blue eyes trying to cut you out. Won't you give me some money now?"

After this, she later told Martin:

"Give me all you have got - watch, money, and rings," adding, "Tomorrow morning I will bring you your planet and a true, living photo of your young man, together with

· LA·MOVREV ·

that of the dark-eyed girl who is trying to deceive you. He is the man that you love, and one that you're going to marry."

Florence Martin had some doubts about this, and replied to the fortune-teller:

"I may love him, but not enough to marry him."

But Kate Smith was well used to dealing with such objections and answered:

"But I'll, show you the photo of the one that you *are* going to marry. Get all that you've got; place it in your hand with a good wish, and pass it into mine. I will return you all the things on Saturday. All that I shall charge you for my trouble will be sixpence. That won't break you, will it?"

In this case, Florence Martin showed she had better judgment than the women in the previous cases, and after agreeing to see Smith when she returned, called the police.

Smith received one month's imprisonment, with hard labour.

WITCHCRAFT..?

Of the many other cases of fortune-telling in the local newspapers, one report subtitled *A Sixpenny Love Charm* shows how fortune-telling slipped easily into the casting of spells, of which the courts most definitely disapproved.

In this case, defendant Sarah Mann demanded sixpence so that a love spell might have an extra ingredient:

The Clerk.—Did she say what it was for?
Witness.—She said, "The dragon's blood to put on the paper costs sixpence." (Laughter).
The Clerk.—What did she say the dragon's blood was for?
Witness.—To draw the young men on the wish paper. (Loud laughter). She also said she should want some more money for the loving cup. She had been in the house four times before. I refused to give her any money, and she became very abusive and called me bad names.

Sarah Mann was an inconsistent figure. On her arrest for fortune-telling, she told the detective "I know I can't tell fortunes; it was only a little bit of fun." Yet, while she was being held at the station, she told the same detective that if he would "fetch the teapot" she would tell his fortune by tea-leaves...

The prisoner denied fortune-telling, but the magistrates sentenced her to seven days' imprisonment with hard labour.

BAD LUCK

Fear was a useful tool for some fortune-tellers. Another report from the *Portsmouth Evening News* in 1899, tells how one Amelia Small terrified one of her clients out of her belongings, after asking her for various metal objects.

Her duped client handed Small a gun-metal watch and a chain made of Chinese silver. The prisoner then crossed her hand with the objects in the usual way, and informed her that she would get into a better business in the first quarter of the coming year. However, when her client asked Small for her belongings back...

She said she could not give witness her money and watch and chain back again as it would bring her very dreadful luck. Witness said that prisoner terrified her very much at the time. Finally, the prisoner took her departure with the money, watch and chain, and a table cover.

Scaring gullible people can be a lucrative business!

THE SCIENCE OF PALMISTRY

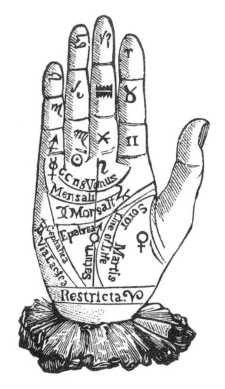

Fortune-telling by fraudsters who wanted to trick as much money from their victims as possible was a common problem in Portsmouth, but what of those who offered a service to clients who came to them willingly? And what of those who offered palmistry because they genuinely believed in it? Whether or not it was possible to read the future, was it fair to group those who honestly believed they were providing a service with those cynically manipulating the gullible and superstitious for their cash? Or were the two groups really doing the same thing? The law made no distinction, even if "respectable" fortune-tellers believed there was one.

PALMISTRY LECTURES AT SOUTHSEA

Some people hoped they could bring scientific discipline to fortune-telling.

On 10th November 1897, the *Portsmouth Evening News* reported on an event in Southsea that tried to do so:

There was a good attendance at the lecture on "Scientific Palmistry," delivered in the small Portland Hall on Tuesday afternoon by Mrs. St. Hill, President of the London Chirological Society, and authoress of several works on the subject.

In the course of her lecture, which was illustrated by limelight photographs of the hands of famous men, and of typical cases in the London Hospitals, Mrs St Hill explained that the object of the Society was to clear palmistry from the accumulations of superstition and rubbish which have been allowed to cover it, so that it has come to be regarded for the most part simply as a means of fortune-telling and humbug, and to place it on

a sure foundation as an exact science. She claimed that the individual character might be gauged from a study of the lines on the palm and also from the shape and outline of the hand, and argued that it would be a great assistance to parents in the education of their children and in choosing trades and professions for them. She contended that the existence of a subtle connection between the lines in the hand and the action of the brain was very clearly shown by the cases of paralysis and concussion, in which the lines fade entirely out of the hand. A second lecture by Mrs. St. Hill is announced for Friday evening next.

Could palmistry ever be elevated to a science, as Mrs St Hill hoped? In the Portland Hall it might have seemed possible, but out in the world beyond - not at all!

BUSINESS AS USUAL

It was business as usual between palmists and the police. In the *Portsmouth Evening News* of 18th July 1901, a technique for catching a higher class of fortune-teller was revealed when three palmists were tried on the same day. The first prisoner before the court was the romantically named Madame Valma, whose real name was the slightly less romantic Ethel Freeman.

The reporter, who had clearly taken a shine to her, described her as "an attractive-looking woman with fair hair" who "wore a tasteful light jacket and a sailor hat, and was accommodated with a seat in the dock."

"A ROGUE AND A VAGABOND"

The witnesses in Madame Valma's case were both wives of borough firemen: Mrs Selina Cottrell and Mrs Wilson, who had attended a sitting with her. Cottrell described how a card in the defendant's window read "Madame Valma, Palmist" and that she had been invited in and her fortune read in her palms for a shilling.

Valma's defence was very much the one Mrs. St Hill had outlined in her lecture - that palmistry was not fortune-telling but was in fact a science that revealed the character. However, the fact that Valma had told the women how long they would live, that Mrs Wilson's life would be full of trouble till the age of 35, and even that she should avoid going on the water, appeared to be stretching the character profiling a bit far.

Madame Valma was found guilty and adjudged a rogue and a vagabond under the 1824 Vagrancy Act, for which she was fined £5 and 5s costs, with the alternative of 21 days' imprisonment. She paid immediately.

The story was the same for the next defendant, Madame Burton, aka Albertha Louisa Bodie, who had been visited by the same women. She claimed to be a music-hall artist, but made her living solely from fortune-telling, pleading that she had no other means of income. Once again, £5 5s was the fine imposed, and she was also pronounced a rogue and a vagabond.

The final case was against Mr Wynne Blanchard, who styled himself "The American Professor". Just as before with the others, he claimed he was a palmist and didn't tell fortunes, asserting that palmistry was a science and that he simply divined character through it. Once more, he was declared a rogue and a vagabond and fined £5, 5s.

A STRIKING COINCIDENCE

It appeared a cut-and-dried case that three fraudsters had been convicted. However, the report in the *Portsmouth Evening News* noted something unusual about them. "Curiously enough," it commented, the fortunes cast by these three separate palmists "were somewhat similar ".

Was it a coincidence that in all three cases, the predictions made were that Mrs Cottrell would live to a ripe old age, "but would soon be left a widow?" It would be fascinating to find out if that were true!

A BENT LITTLE MAN

A similar story was reported in the *Hampshire Telegraph* for 3rd September 1926, in which "Professor" Walter D'Auburne

was tried for fortune-telling. Described as a "bent little man" of no more than four foot tall, he was fined 10s for "4s worth of prophecies". The police had sent out a police matron as witness, who reported that he had predicted her age at death and that she would have an offer of marriage.

D'Auburne's personal circumstances echo those of some of the other defendants. He stated that he and his wife "were both respectable people under straitened circumstances," and he claimed to know many of the respectable people of the town as evidence of this.

A WASTE OF POLICE TIME?

More such cases were reported in the *Portsmouth Evening News*, over the years. Sometimes the court cases were inadvertently comic, like the 1930 case in which the witness, Mrs Norris, was told by a fortune-teller that "she had a good husband but he was very difficult to understand and manage and would probably go abroad." When asked by the clerk at court if this was true about her husband being difficult to understand and manage, the world-weary voice of the long-suffering wife can be heard in her reply:

"I think all men are."

Mrs Norris was told by the defendant palmist, a Mrs. Pollard, that she should be wary of a fair woman who was likely to come between her and her husband, and she was even invited to toss a crystal and make a wish. Once again, the move into spell-casting is a short one, and certainly did nothing for her case in the eyes of the court.

Mrs Pollard's defence was that she and her entire family were living close to poverty, with her husband an invalid. She said she'd applied for parish relief but was denied it because she told fortunes... and so, she was stuck trying to make her living from fortune-telling. She was often bed-bound, and sometimes had to give readings from her sick bed.

A defendant in a later case said she had been earning her living by fortune-telling for 12 years on fairgrounds and other places, and didn't know she was doing anything wrong.

Reading stories like this, one has to wonder, were such prosecutions the best use of police time? Were they worth it? And why? Whether there is any truth in fortune-telling or not, be that by palmistry, tarot cards, crystal-gazing, divination, runes - whatever the technique - as long as no-one is being harmed and everyone consents, was it really the law's business at all?

II

WITCHCRAFT, VAGRANCY AND SPIRITUALISM

COMMUNING WITH SPIRITS

One group for whom the law on fortune-telling and divination presented a real problem was the Spiritualists.

Just like fortune-tellers, Spiritualists were frequently accused of preying on the gullible and delivering fake messages from beyond the grave through "conjuration", which was still illegal under a far older law than the Vagrancy Act - the 1735 Witchcraft Act.

Yet calling on spirits was central to their religion, they argued, and had been from the beginning of the movement.

SPIRITS ON THE RISE

Modern Spiritualism started in 1847 in Hydesville, New York, when three girls, the Fox sisters, claimed to be able to communicate with spirits. The phenomena of rapping and spirit manifestations they demonstrated drew a huge audience, and what started as a small community sensation grew into a fully realised religion.

In the aftermath of the mass deaths of the American Civil War, millions sought solace in communication with their deceased loved ones and demand for the Fox sisters grew.

They toured the United States and Europe, creating converts and inspiring new mediums along the way.

Soon the religion of Spiritualism was established in Britain, where some leading scientists became convinced there was truth in these spiritual phenomena. Disembodied voices, tables rising off the ground with no observable support, and precise details drawn from the private lives of the deceased that convinced their living relatives gave Spiritualism credibility in their eyes.

Its critics, however, described it as cheap trickery or necromancy - and accused mediums of either the very same tricks used by fortune-tellers and self-proclaimed scientific palmists, or of conjuring evil spirits.

Supporters and critics of the new religion of Spiritualism argued over it with the most passionate language.

PROMINENT PORTSMOUTH JUDGE

Just so when the editor of the *Hampshire Telegraph* discovered a prominent Portsmouth judge, Serjeant Cox, Recorder of Portsmouth, had converted to the faith. To the editor's annoyance, Cox supported a leading figure in the movement, D D Home, whom the *Hampshire Telegraph* described as a "notorious Spiritualist".

An editorial entitled *The Portsmouth Recorder with D D Home, The Spiritualist* published on 22nd July 1871 mocked Serjeant Cox for believing Home could psychically move tables so that they "skipped round the apartment like rocks and woods at the lute of Orpheus; whilst shadow hands... quiver above the heads of the company." The editor was

clearly offended by the whole business, and went on to describe the supposed phenomena Home had displayed:

Mr. Home's person was "levitated," or raised in the air to the very ceiling, and his friends insist that on one occasion he passed in this way out of one window and in at another. A still more remarkable fact remains to be told. Mr. Home suffered elongation, his stature was increased by several inches, and shortly afterwards contracted to his original size.

In the presence of Dr. Crookes, Dr. Higgins, and Serjeant Cox, an accordion was placed in a sort of cage under a table, and Mr. Home caused it to play a tune while touching it only with the tips of the fingers of one hand. The observer, it is said, satisfied himself that neither Mr. Home's other hand nor his feet assisted in producing sound from the accordion.

CONVICTED FRAUDSTER

The editorial noted that Serjeant Cox believed in these phenomena despite Home having once been convicted for defrauding an elderly lady of her fortune by persuading her he'd contacted her dead husband. The article mocked Serjeant Cox, claiming the psychic experiments he observed were actually "experiments upon the capacity of mankind for yielding to any pretention which is at once new and bold".

The article dismissed Spiritualism, the writer making it absolutely clear he believed Serjeant Cox to have been deceived, and that he was possibly a bit mad, a complete idiot - or both.

SOUTHSEA'S FIRM BELIEVERS

Believers remained unswayed by such angry attacks. Spiritualism in Portsmouth thrived during the 1880s and 1890s, at the same time that Arthur Conan Doyle was working as a GP in Elm Grove, Southsea. He was part of a highly active and engaged group of Spiritualist seekers-of-truth, performing countless experiments to uncover the secrets of the paranormal.

Conan Doyle moved in strange and esoteric circles in Portsmouth. Though he started off as a sceptic, his friend Major-General Alfred Wilkes Drayson encouraged him to take the possibility of spirit communication seriously. So it was that Doyle came to believe it was his scientific duty to investigate spiritual phenomena.

Through Drayson's circle, Doyle met A P Sinnet in Southsea. Sinnet was the right-hand-man of Madame Blavatsky, a Russian aristocrat-turned-spiritual guide who claimed to be in contact with The Masters of Ancient Wisdom - mystic beings she said had sent her to Tibet for spiritual instruction. Madame Blavatsky was co-founder of the mystical group called the Theosophical Society, and a major occult figure in the later half of the 19th Century. And here was her influence falling upon Conan Doyle at Major-General Alfred Wilkes-Drayson's gatherings in Southsea.

A SÉANCE

When another military man, Lieutenant-General Thomas Harward invited Conan Doyle to attend a séance held on 24th January 1887 at Kingston Lodge in the north of Portsmouth, he agreed to sit in with an open and enquiring mind. The group comprised Doyle, his new wife, Louise, Henry Ball (a friend with whom he'd been doing experiments in telepathy), Lieutenant-General Harward and Nancy Harward, the general's 22-year-old daughter.

They began with a reading from the *First Book of Ezekiel*, in which a spirit appears before the Prophet. Then the lights were dimmed and the séance began. After much waiting, the group finally received a message. It read: "You are going too slowly; how long are you going to take?"

Doyle was not impressed by his early Portsmouth paranormal experiments. He recalled in his later autobiographical work, *Memories And Adventures*:

They sat around a dining-room table which after a time, their hands being upon it, began to sway and finally got sufficient motion to tap with one leg. They then asked questions and received answers, more or less wise and more or less to the point. They were got by the tedious process of reciting the alphabet and writing down the letter which the tap indicated. It seemed to me that we were collectively pushing the table and that our own wills were concerned in bringing down the leg at the right moment.

A MESSAGE FROM BEYOND

Nevertheless, further séances followed. During one, a message came through for Nancy from her cousin, Henry Hastie, who had died three years earlier, "I have not nor ever shall forget you, darling little Nancy. Please love another for my sake. Henry Hastie."

As the message was received, Doyle noted that the temperature in the room plummeted and Nancy Harward "became icy cold and experienced a sensation as of soft hands patting her upon the palm with a strong feeling that someone was standing behind her. At the command of the spirits we discontinued the sitting."

CONVERSION

Doyle attended 20 sittings with this group, but remained unconvinced he was experiencing anything unusual until he invited a medium, a Mr Horstead, to give a sitting in the summer of 1887. He was so impressed by the results that he wrote his letter to *Light* magazine mentioned earlier in this book.

The letter revealed exactly what clinched it for him:

Last week I was invited by two friends to join them in a sitting with an old gentleman who was reputed to have considerable mediumistic power. It was the first time that I had ever had the opportunity of sitting with anyone who was not a novice and inquirer like myself. I may remark here that for some days I had been debating in my mind whether I should get a copy of Leigh Hunt's Comic Dramatists of the Restoration — the question being whether the mental pollution arising from Messrs. Congreve, Wycherley, and Co. would be compensated for by the picture of the manners and customs of those days to be gathered from their pages, and which I had particular reasons for wishing to be well up in. I had thought the matter over, but had dismissed it from my mind a day or two before the séance. On sitting, our medium came quickly under control, and delivered a trance address, containing much interesting and elevating matter. He then became clairvoyant, describing one or two scenes which we had no opportunity of testing. So far, the meeting had been very interesting, but not above the possibility of deception. We then proposed writing. The medium took up a pencil, and after a few convulsive movements, he wrote a message to each of us. Mine ran: "This gentleman is a healer. Tell him from me not to read Leigh Hunt's book." Now, sir, I can swear that no one knew I had contemplated reading that book, and, moreover, it was no case of thought-reading, for I had never referred to the matter all day. I can only say that if I had had to devise a test message I could not have hit upon one which was so absolutely inexplicable on any hypothesis except that held by Spiritualists.

Doyle believed that something had actively probed his mind, and concluded that it was a spirit of some sort. It was the start of his great journey in Spiritualism that would eventually lead him to proclaim the reality of ghosts, telepathy, mediumship, poltergeists, divining, spirit photography and, yes, even fairies.

He went on to be a founder member of the Hampshire Society for Psychical Research, a member of the Ghost Club and of the London-based Society for Psychical Research. In later life he published numerous books on the paranormal and became one of the leaders of the early 20th Century Spiritualist movement; he was elected president of the London Spiritualists' Alliance (the leading Spiritualist organisation in Britain) and dedicated the final ten years of his life to Spiritualist missionary work around the world.

CONAN DOYLE: LEADER OF THE SPIRITUALISTS

Doyle did return to Portsmouth from time to time. In 1916, after he announced to the world his firm belief in Spiritualism he embarked on a series of talks around the country to spread the word. In September 1919 he spoke in The Portland Hall, Southsea, to a capacity audience of 1600 on the subject of *Death and the Hereafter*. It was during this visit that he attended a séance and became convinced he had spoken with the spirit of his deceased son, Kingsley, who died in the Great War. Doyle also gave a talk at the Spiritualist Temple on Victoria Road South in 1926.

He was a tireless missionary for Spiritualism. In 1930, just a week before his death, he led a deputation of the "United Spiritualist Organisations" to the Home Secretary to ask for the amendment of the Witchcraft and Vagrancy Acts under which fortune-tellers (like those in the previous chapter) and mediums were liable for prosecution...

It is fascinating to think that his spiritualist trajectory was launched thanks to psychic investigations in a seaside resort in the 1880s in the very same year Sherlock Holmes entered the world.

HORACE LEAF - SPIRITUALIST LECTURER

Doyle was not the only Spiritualist to address the people of Portsmouth in the aftermath of the Great War. Numerous other well-known lecturers - though perhaps not superstars like Sir Arthur Conan Doyle - came to the town during the massive outpouring of national grief after the Armistice.

In 1920, one such figure was Horace Leaf, whose presence sparked debate about the truth of Spiritualism. On 16th March, 1920, the *Portsmouth Evening News* reported he had come to talk at the Portland Hall, Southsea, where he was welcomed by local vicar, the Rev. Bruce Cornford.

Cornford was clearly an open-minded Christian who recognised that while there were good and bad Christians, there were also good and bad Spiritualists. Whilst he didn't necessarily agree with everything in Spiritualism, he didn't see why Christians should not hold out the hand of friendship to Spiritualists, and he welcomed Leaf to the lectern at the talk.

GHOSTS IN SOLID FORM

Horace Leaf's lecture was about spirit manifestations, which is why the report in the paper was wonderfully entitled *Ghosts In Solid Form*. Leaf explained that there were 30 or 40 different ways in which spirits communicated with this world "in a direct and scientific manner", but the most remarkable

method was the phenomenon of physical materialisation, which occurred when a supposed spiritual substance called *ectoplasm* was exuded by mediums. This substance then took on physical form and complete living entities were created from it.

Leaf spoke about the work of Dr Crawford, a Belfast engineer who had studied the ectoplasmic manifestations of the teenage medium Kathleen Goligher, and of the experiments of chemist Sir William Crookes on the manifestations of Florence Cook, who had apparently summoned an entire, solid spirit known as Katie King. The article commented:

Many slides were shown of photographs of materialised spirit forms, and Mr. Leaf, in the course of his explanatory remarks, laid stress on the exhaustive scientific investigations of Dr. Crawford... The concluding series were the sensational pictures of Katie King, whose actual form appeared on many occasions to the late Mr William Crookes, through the medium, Florence Cook.

Crookes was, Leaf noted, a renowned scientist who was initially sceptical about the manifestations of Katie King, but once convinced by their reality had kept to his views despite the effect on his reputation in the scientific community. He finished with a quote from Sir Arthur Conan Doyle (who once described Crookes's photographs as "the most wonderful in the world"), saying, "I have never known a materialist who has become a spiritualist return to materialism, and have never known a spiritualist become a materialist."

WITCHCRAFT AND SPIRITUALISM

The newspaper report was accompanied by another of a lecture held at the Garrison Church, Old Portsmouth, by the Rev. A. Davenport Kelly, M.A., of Kelham Theological College.

Kelham compared the supposedly new phenomena of Spiritualism with witchcraft, and said that while the phenomena in themselves were not new, their scientific investigation was.

"And there was need for that investigation," he added, "because there was a tendency in the human mind to accept the marvellous for the miraculous."

The research, he added, had concluded there was very little truth in manifestations and other physical or material phenomena. As for those Spiritualists who weren't fraudulent, well, clearly they were using "telepathy".

He went on to explain that while telepathy was not yet fully understood, Spiritualist phenomena could be put down to "telepathy operating much more freely where a person

was in a trance, or subconscious state, which was often the case at a Spiritualist séance."

Davenport's reliance on other paranormal phenomenon in order to argue against Spiritualism seems a weakness in his argument! Nevertheless he continued with the valid point that there were very few cases of really useful information given by alleged spirits, adding "How helpful it would be to Scotland Yard, for instance, if in the case of murder, Mrs. Piper, or some other prominent medium, could get in touch with the spirit of the victim. The police would be saved a lot of trouble!"

GOOD AND BAD SPIRITS

Yet another local lecture was given at the same time at St. Michael's Church, Southsea, by Father A E Monahan, Vicar of Monmouth, on the dangers of Spiritualism.

Monahan was a firm Anglo-Catholic with unbending views who saw evil in this young religion that had found a new audience since the Great War. "Spiritualism," he said, "had not been created by the war. People had only to consult *The Bible* to find that there had been always a temptation in the storm and stress of war to resort to occult inquiries."

His argument was rather that if you accepted that the phenomena were real, "that did not make them right, because there were good and evil spirits."

He believed there was evil at work in Spiritualism. Those places where the conjuring of the dead appeared in *The*

WITCH of ENDOR

352

Bible included the story of the Witch of Endor whom Saul consulted to summon the spirit of the Prophet Samuel in much the same way modern Spiritualists claimed to do.

Since Saul only resorted to the witch after being abandoned by God, Monahan's argument was essentially that people attending séances were being tricked by the devil.

JOURNALIST ATTENDS SÉANCE

Spiritualists were often arrested and tried for tricking people out of their money or to gain influence, and yet, séances continued because grieving relatives in the post-war years sought to contact their departed relatives. One intrepid reporter for the *Portsmouth Evening News* decided to attend a séance and write about it in an article of 24th June 1932.

I reprint the main section below because it is so full of wide-eyed wonder at the events of that evening, and an almost complete absence of critical thinking.

The séance was held with the medium Mr L B Lilley whom we met before channelling the spirit of Dickens, his son, five women and three men at 72 Oriel Road, Portsmouth.

After sitting down in the dark at a table on which were placed the trumpets through which the spirits spoke, there was a brief moment of hymn singing, some adjusting of the lighting to make it dark enough for spirit activity... and soon the spirits started to come through:

"JOCK"

After about, as I should judge, three or four minutes, a warning S-s-h!" from someone in the circle brought silence, and for me the first thrill of the evening came.

A voice, Scottish in accent and rather unusually guttural, with a slightly metallic sound, hit the intense darkness. It was "Jock," one of the controls—I think that is the correct term—who had come through."

He was in a jovial mood, friendly and helpful in his response to the salutations of those of the circle, of whom he was obviously an old acquaintance. There was so much cordiality and friendliness about his remarks and his voice that a slight feeling of apprehension I had been experiencing vanished.

I could not follow all that he said. His Scotch was extremely broad.

When Jock came the circle changed from hymns to popular Scottish ditties such as "I love a lassie" and "Auld Lang Syne," which he evidently enjoyed, even joining in himself. "Swanee River" was also sung.

Mr A G Pawsey, one of the circle, asked Jock what line he should take regarding his desire to progress with the work in which he was deeply interested. Jock replied with a chuckle, that all he had to do was to take a pencil, draw a line and there he had it!

SCOTTISH ALL RIGHT

Another specimen of Jock's pawky humour was his comment on Mr. Lilley senior's observation that he often retailed Jock's jokes to his friends. Jock asked him how much he got for them.

But the lighter side was only an interlude, and Jock replied to several queries for members of the circle and also prayed. Thus, a lady asked if her father might give a message through Jock, and another wanted to know if she might hope to get in touch with her deceased husband. The first request was granted, and the father spoke to the daughter. To the second request Jock replied that she must be patient and wait longer.

During all this there were occasional noises of thumping, and once something tapped me several times on the top of the head. It felt like one of the trumpets, and indeed, I was informed afterwards that this was what it was. The tapping, it seemed, was a friendly gesture on the part of Jock. Others received a like salutation, but not all. We had been favoured.

At intervals Jock urged us to sing up, which we did very briskly at times.

A GERMAN'S REQUEST

Suddenly there was a hush. Jock informed us that a German spirit desired to convey a message. It was to the effect, so far as I can remember, that he wanted to get in touch with another son of Mr. Lilley's, whose chum was killed alongside him in an air raid in London. The German spirit was hoping that by this means he might obtain the forgiveness of the man his bomb had killed.

Mr. and Mrs. Lilley were also informed that the son in London would shortly be coming on a visit, and that he would experience a change of spirit.

Jock was with us much longer than White Cloud, a Red Indian control. Before this Indian came Jock warned us not to be frightened.

The warning was not out of season, for when White Cloud came he let off a loud "Ha! Ha! Ha!" that made at least one of the company leap in his chair. White Cloud could not, however, be induced to go in for a lengthy conversation.

Peggy was another brief visitant from the Beyond who did not stay long. Before the séance ended the Rev. Mr Deakin. another control who comes at times said a few consolatory words. In earth life, apparently, he was a Church of England clergyman in the North of England.

It had been hoped that Charles Dickens would speak through the medium, as we were told he had done on previous occasions, but in this the Circle last night was disappointed.

MARSHALL HALL

Other spiritual voices which from time to time have spoken through Mr. Lilley, so I am told, are Sir Edward Marshall Hall, and Father Damien, who prayed in Latin.

Mr. Lilley also told me afterwards that they had had considerable success on occasions with phenonema,

and that once an illuminated cross had been seen to move right round the room. Members of the circle had frequently been touched on the body.

When Dickens spoke at one séance. Mr. Lilley Senr. said he addressed him as "Sir" and Dickens asked him why he should take the trouble to do that, all being equal in social standing, if not in spiritual advancement.

It should be added that Mr, Lilley, jnr does not confine his work to his own home, but takes part as a medium in séances in other places. Like most earnest participants in the work of Spiritualism, he deplores the undeniable fraud which exists, and which brings discredit on the movement; and he points out that their own people are the first to denounce such when discovered.

"I believe," he said in conclusion, "that this movement in the years to come will sweep the world."

So came an end to the séance attended by a keen *Portsmouth Evening News* reporter in the summer of 1932.

As we shall see in the next chapter, those who promised communion with the dead were doomed to meet far more resistance than the medium Mr Lilley jnr imagined.

12
HELEN DUNCAN AND THE "LAST WITCH TRIAL"

"CONVICTED OF WITCHCRAFT"

When you tell people who haven't heard the story of the last woman to be imprisoned under the 1735 Witchcraft Act in the UK, the first thing you hear is shock at the date it happened.

"1944!?!" they gasp in disbelief.

And yet it's true. The last person to be jailed under the Witchcraft Act was tried in the closing years of World War 2. Her name was Helen Duncan, and she was arrested at a séance in Portsmouth.

The 1735 Witchcraft Act isn't all it sounds. The law was introduced during the reign of George II to replace previous laws dealing with women accused of necromancy and other magical practices. Since Enlightenment attitudes no longer recognised the reality of magic, the Witchcraft Act was designed to deal with those preying on the credulity of others.

The wording of the Act reveals its real purpose. It punished those who "*pretended* to conjure spirits" rather than acknowledging that they *actually* performed magic. The introduction of the Witchcraft Act meant the law no longer recognied "real" witches.

In 1824, the act was accompanied by the Vagrancy Act, which we saw in action in the chapter on fortune-telling.

While the Vagrancy Act carried a maximum three month prison sentence, the older Witchcraft Act could result in up to a year's incarceration. Essentially, then, Helen Duncan was tried not for witchcraft, but for fraud.

THE BELIEVER'S VIEW

The story of the events leading up to the arrest of Helen Duncan are told markedly differently by those who believe in her powers and those who don't.

Believers will tell you Helen Duncan was an established and respected medium who for years had been contacting the deceased. She was part of the Spiritualist upsurge that occurred in the late 19th and early 20th Centuries.

After the Great War, mediums were very much in demand, and with the Second World War, once again their ability to reconnect people with lost loved ones provided solace for the bereaved.

In early December 1941, Helen Duncan held a séance at the grandly named Master Temple Psychic Centre, in fact a small room over a shop at 301 Copnor Road, Portsmouth. She received a message from a dead sailor who wanted to let a relative know he had passed on safely to the afterlife after he had died during the sinking of the Royal Navy battleship *HMS Barham*.

This is quite a common example of the type of message mediums passed on to loved ones at the time. However, in this case there was a problem. Although *HMS Barham* had been sunk on 26th November 1941, the Government had suppressed news of the disaster for propaganda purposes. Thus, it was impossible for Duncan to have known about it through conventional means. Which left the question - how did she know the *Barham* had sunk?

The case came to the attention of Royal Naval intelligence officers. Was Duncan receiving spirit messages from the

"other side", or, more likely, was she a spy passing on information to undermine morale? The case was noted, but not investigated.

Oblivious to Establishment interest, Duncan continued holding séances up and down the country, including in Portsmouth. Then, in the build-up to D-Day, seeking to keep plans to invade mainland Europe secret, the Government felt it was time to silence Helen Duncan.

This, at least, is how believers tell the story.

WHAT WE KNOW FOR SURE

The events leading up to the arrest of Duncan are as follows.

Toward the end of 1943 RN officer Lieutenant Stanley Worth went under cover to investigate the activities of the Master Temple Psychic Centre. Mrs Homer, who worked at the Centre, told Lieutenant Worth that Mrs Duncan could produce spirits, and that her spirit guide appeared via the mysterious material known as ectoplasm, which the medium exuded from her eyes, ears, nose and mouth, manifesting a solid spirit. Mrs Duncan charged 12s 6d for each attendee.

Lieutenant Worth asked if he could bring along a sceptical friend, Lieutenant Fowler, and was told yes, but that he must not touch the ectoplasm or it would rush back inside Mrs Duncan's body with such force it might kill her. Mrs Homer claimed that Mrs Duncan had once had an operation and inside her body were found cigarette ends, matchsticks and all sorts of other items, that had been dragged in with the ectoplasm. At the trial the prosecution mockingly compared the effect to "a vacuum cleaner."

DETAILS FROM THE WITCHCRAFT TRIAL

Newspaper reports of Helen Duncan's trial reveal the details of the séances Lieutenant Worth attended.

At one séance, Lieutenants Worth and Fowler sat with others in a darkened room lit by a red light. People were asked to surrender any torches.

Helen Duncan was seated in a curtained-off part of the room. As soon as the curtains were closed, a voice began to speak in the darkness, and a white form appeared. Mrs Homer informed the room that this was Albert, Duncan's spirit guide.

Albert announced that there was a spirit waiting to talk to someone, and Lieutenant Worth asked "Are you my Aunt?" The spirit replied "Yes", which the prosecution commented was "unfortunate, because all Mr Worth's aunts are alive."

Later, Albert claimed to have contact with a mutilated boy. When a woman in the audience identified him as hers, she was invited to come forward in the darkness and touch what was said to be the stump of his arm.

Other events that night included Albert saying he wanted to "come to somebody who had put their foot on an animal." To this, a woman in the audience revealed she had put an injured cat out of its misery in this way. In response, the cat briefly manifested and miaowed.

Next came the form of a policemen, of which another woman in the audience asked, "Is that you, dad?" The figure replied, "Wait a moment while I put on my helmet."

After Albert retired, a female entity called Peggy, who had a strong Scottish, accent was called. She sang the Scottish song "Loch Lomond" for Lieutenant Fowler, and then announced she was leaving.

Next, the audience was shown a parrot called Bronco who said "Pretty Polly", and then heard a voice which Mrs Homer identified as her granny. This entity sang a song in an unidentified language.

Another entity to appear that night was a Yorkshireman, who approached the audience and bent over and shook hands with someone in the second row. This entity claimed that he did not think much of Mrs Duncan because she was too fat!

Lieutenant Fowler was disgusted by what he was sure was cheap trickery and reported it to the police. His attitude to this séance was echoed by the prosecution barrister, Mr Maude K C, who told the court: "If the prosecution's case is proved, we shall have drawn the curtains back in the Master Temple, and the mockery of the dead will have ceased in the little room above Mr Homer's shop.

STRUGGLE
IN THE DARK

On the night of Duncan's arrest, Lieutenant Worth attended the séance with Police Constable Cross. It was at the point that a white-shrouded form appeared and stood between the curtains that Cross made a lunge and took a grip on it, while Worth produced his torch. In the court case, Cross claimed he had taken hold of Mrs Duncan, who struggled so much that a white shroud she was wearing was torn from his hands. Worth claimed to see Mrs Duncan trying to get rid of a piece of white material, but then, someone knocked the torch out of his hand. Everyone jumped up and there was pandemonium. Worth says he briefly saw Mrs Duncan standing in her bare feet trying to put on her shoes. Soon after she started screaming that she was ill and that she wanted a doctor.

Constable Cross told everyone to keep still and then blew his police whistle, which was the signal for a police inspector to come in. In the search afterwards, the white cloth, the material evidence of fraud, was not found.

A WITCH TRIAL!

Helen Duncan and her three accomplices, Mrs Francis Brown and Mr and Mrs Homer were arrested. In fact, Mrs Homer was really Elizabeth Jones: the couple were not married, a fact the newspapers reported as evidence of their disreptable nature. They were first held under the 1824 Vagrancy Act, but this was later changed to a charge of conspiracy. Finally it was decided to charge them with contravention of Section 4 of the Witchcraft Act, 1735, which states that anyone who "may pretend to exercise or use any kind of witchcraft, sorcery or conjuration" is liable to imprisonment.

The Defence's case was essentially that Helen Duncan was not *pretending* to exercise such powers, she *really did* have these powers. To prove it, the court was asked to allow a demonstration of Duncan's psychic phenomena to the jury. All that would be required would be a few moments for Mrs Duncan to "tranquilise her mind" and a bare naked room with a small portion curtained off.

But the Recorder replied dismissively: "There is no use wasting the time of the jury witnessing some kind of demonstration."

Without the chance to demonstrate her power, the defence produced 15 witnesses, who all attested to Mrs Duncan's ability to manifest real psychic phenomena.

WITNESSES TO
PSYCHIC PHENOMENA

One such witness, Alfred Dodd, a psychic investigator for 40 years, testified how, 12 years before in Manchester, Mrs Duncan had manifested the form of his own grandfather. He said he was "very corpulent," and "looked round the room very critically until his eyes caught mine." Next, he "strode across the room, put out his hand and grasped mine, saying 'I am very pleased to see you here in my native city.'"

Dodd claimed his grandfather was wearing the smoking cap he used to wear, was dressed in a dark suit, and had a "donkey-fringe" beard. He told Dodd "I am sorry you're having a rough time." Dodd explained that at that time he had lost property. His grandfather added later, "Keep your pecker up, old boy, never say die while there is a shot in the locker."

Dodd then claimed his grandfather "held my hand so firmly that it ached for hours afterwards," and that later his grandfather smacked his own chest three times and said: "It's solid, Alfred."

Dodd also claimed to have seen the ghost of his first sweetheart, Helen, who died when she was 21.

"She stood, she waved in exactly the same way she did when I took her home after the last social dance. She came and stood before me, a living palpitating woman, the same hair I knew so well - dark and ruddy - the same eyes, hazel and shining with animation. She was so real that instinctively I put my arms out to her, thinking she would be solid, but she started back saying 'Don't touch me.' and faded before my eyes. She dulled into nothing. That is the truth. She passed over in 1897."

Another witness, James William Herries, a psychic investigator for 20 years and a personal friend of Sir Arthur Conan Doyle claimed Duncan had materialised Doyle's spirit: "The figure was a little ghostly, but I easily recognised the rounded features of Sir Arthur, particularly the moustache. The figure spoke, and I traced a distinct similarity to Arthur's voice."

These and other testimonies bore no weight in the court room, however. The case was concerned with the events of the night of the séance and nothing else. Furthermore, since the law assumed it was impossible to conjure spirits, the fact she even claimed to do so meant she *must* be guilty.

The jury took half an hour to deliberate. Helen Duncan was found guilty and sentenced to nine months in prison.

Upon the sentence being delivered, she cried out:

"I have done nothing; is there a God?"

CONTROVERSY

These, then, are the facts of the case that led Helen Duncan to become the last person to be jailed under the 1735 Witchcraft Act. One more woman was convicted under the act the same year. Frail and elderly, Jane Rebecca Yorke of Forest Gate was not imprisoned but bound over to keep the peace.

The arguments that continue to rage about Helen Duncan centre around two main points - was she a fraud, and if so why was the Establishment so interested in her?

Her followers believe she was arrested because she had revealed the sinking of the *Barham*, and might have revealed other secrets in the build-up to D-Day. The authorities couldn't let that happen, they argue, and silenced her.

Those on the other side of the argument say it was a moral duty to stop Duncan abusing the gullible, and had nothing to do with her supposed powers. In this telling of the story, Duncan is a serial conwoman who deserved everything she got. Calling her an egomaniac from childhood, they say she was caught cheating and lying throughout her career. Indeed, flash photographs (below) of her control, Albert, reveal crude dummies, while the supposed ectoplasm she manifested was made of cheesecloth, or egg white mixed with other chemicals.

Others again claim that news about *HMS Barham* had slipped out to a few relatives and was known - though this, again, is denied by others

Yet the fact remains, Helen Duncan *did* indeed talk about the sinking of the *Barham* before it was made public...

How she came to know about it remains a mystery for believers and non-believers to argue over for years to come!

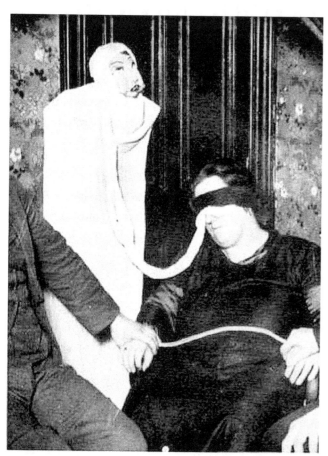

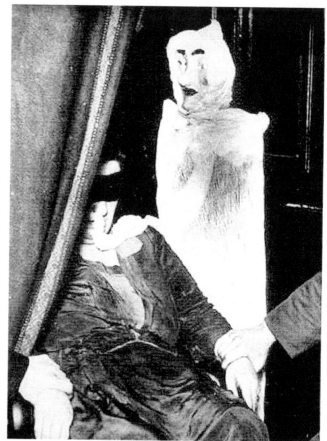

13
GHOST SHIPS
AND
HAUNTED SHIPS

SEA
SPIRITS

From reports of *HMS BARHAM* and a disaster at sea, we move to the mysteries that lie in the deep and out on the ever-moving seas...

The vastness and the unpredictability of the ocean have always made it a home for superstition and stories of the uncanny and strange. Such tales include not only sirens and mermaids, but beings of ill omen, such as the Jonah, who brings his curse to a ship until he leaves it, or Davy Jones, the sailors' very own devil, described by Tobias Smollet in *The Adventures of Peregrine Pickle* (1751) as having saucer eyes, three rows of teeth, horns, a tail, and blue smoke coming from his nostrils.

Indeed, ships can be isolated, eerie entities, as a report in the *Portsmouth Evening News* on 23rd December 1952 related. It described *HMS Formidable* while she was being de-stored. Calling her a "Ghost Ship", it went on:

Sailors who are superstitious— and there are few who are not—will tell you that somewhere on the high seas there are times when the ghost ship, *Mary Celeste*, can still be seen riding the waves and defying even Neptune himself. But every sailor prefers to have more tangible evidence of a ghost ship than the *Mary Celeste*, and that evidence is provided now in Portsmouth Dockyard where the famous war carrier *Formidable* is being de-stored.

Of the eeriness to be found in an empty hulk, the journalist reports:

All dead ships are ghost ships, but *Formidable* has all ingredients and more of the *Mary Celeste*, and when I walked through her deserted messdecks and corridors the other day I had that uncanny feeling, experienced by so many that someone, somewhere, was watching me. At every turning I stopped and listened, and as a chill passed down my spine, I knew it was time to "press on..."

To think: this ship was in the dockyard, being dismantled! How much stranger to meet an empty ship at sea!

THE MARY CELESTE OF MILTON

One genuinely abandoned ship was described by the *Portsmouth Evening News* on the 4th February 1937. Not a ghost ship, but a mystery ship, the writer described how he was taking a walk when he chanced upon the *Zebrina*, which he described as Portsmouth's very own *Mary Celeste*, the famous

ship that was "found mid-ocean, abandoned, with sails set, meals prepared and laid, and never a trace of the crew has ever come to light or the reason for abandoning" her.

Portsmouth's mystery ship used to lie at at the head of Velder Creek, where Milton Common is today.

The owner at time of writing was a Mr. Howard, who had dismantled her masts, and lived aboard with his wife and children. The hold of this medium-sized cargo sailing ship was big enough to be used for boat building and as a motor boat repair depot.

Already two boats had been built within the mystery ship's hold and boats alongside were being converted into motor-boat cabin cruisers. In fact, she was a floating workshop, fully kitted out with electric lights, lathes, circular and band saws and drilling machines, and her three tall pine masts had been cut into lengths ready for sawing into planks to form parts of new sailing or motor boats.

Two children lived with their parents on board, Shirley Ann, aged three and John Frederick, aged 14 months - both of whom had lived their whole lives on board except for three months.

The article described how the *Zebrina* was actually "*Mary Celeste* number two. For she also was drifting or just aground during the Great War off the French coast near Cherbourg, not a soul on board, with all sails set and tables prepared for a meal for the crew."

ZEBRINA AT WAR

So, what was her story? Built at Whitstable in 1873, she was 109 feet long, 185 gross registered tonnage, could carry a cargo of about 300 tons, and was rigged as a threemasted fore and aft schooner, finely made.

Prior to the strange disappearance of her crew in 1917, she had plied her trade on the sea for over 40 years until the Admiralty called on her during the War and she was placed in the King's service. The article went on:

Somewhere in the archives at Whitehall is a record. "*Zebrina*... Found ashore abandoned at Rozel Point, near Dielette, France. October. 1917. Refloated. Settled due to war risk. Crew of five lost." A newspaper cutting states that the little schooner was at Dover on the outbreak of war, was commissioned by the Government, and ran between England and France, until one day she was found derelict and crewless in the Channel. It also records that the master and crew were presumed to have been victims of the enemy...

The article gave further information about her crew and her fate, noting that on the War Memorial erected at Tower

Hill, London by the Imperial War Graves Commission in memory of merchant navy losses, a place of honour is allotted to "our little *Zebrina*, her master and crew, as follows:-"

Zebrina. Faversham. Martin, I. A., Master, Beck, W. H., Bourke. W. E. D., Faus. M., Steward, G.

The *Zebrina*'s log was found on board when she was discovered abandoned, but it gave no help in solving the mysterious affair, apart from listing those on board. The master, Archibald Martin, was 33 years old, the mate. G. Steward, 61, hailing from Brightlingsea. Of the crew, Beck was a London man of 26, Bourke a London boy of 16, and Faus a seaman from Riga, aged 31. The report went on:

PART PLAYED BY FATE

All who were on active service in the War realize what part some refer to as fate played in relation to human life, and it is evidenced here, for it has been found that two men signed off and left *Zebrina* at Appledore, Devon, just before she sailed on her fatal and mysterious voyage, and the Riga seaman signed on and joined the ship.

A log entry shows that she left Falmouth on October 15, 1917 having previously loaded with coal at Swansea. It will be recalled that due to enemy submarine menace at this time a system of convoy by destroyers or armed trawlers was instituted to safeguard merchant shipping crossing from our country to France. It is on record that during October, 1917, there were 217 colliers sailing on one route alone, Penzance to Brest, and of this number only one ship was sunk. These were ships under steam power, and so it is very unlikely that the little sailing ship *Zebrina*, dependent upon the vagaries of wind and tide, with a course relatively shaped and slow speed made would have received advantage by convoy. Under ordinary circumstances, she should have made the crossing in a day or 36 hours, but her arrival port, St. Brieuc, was never reached. Reports state she was found on the French coast on October 17, east of Guernsey, on Rozel Point, practically undamaged, and every member of her crew missing.

SUBMARINE ACTIVITY

The article described how, in her final days, there was much enemy submarine activity in the Channel at this time. Indeed, on October 15th, the day she sailed from Falmouth, a German submarine sank *S.S. Hartburn* off Anvil Point, near Swanage; *S.S. Garthclyde* was sunk off Penzance; a Norwegian vessel, *S.S. Hoode*, was torpedoed off the Ile Baiz; and a Greek steam ship, *Ecaterina*, off Brest. The next day the *St. Paul* and *St. Helens* were sunk in the Bay of Biscay. On the day the *Zebrina* set sail across the Channel she was in reality encircled by enemy submarines.

The weather too was not in her favour, with the period dominated by an almost unbroken record of gales. She thus left Falmouth fully laden and soon encountered gale force winds and heavy squalls. With sea and waves running high, she had only 45 cm / 18 inches of freeboard, that is, distance from waterline to deck. It must have been heavy going.

That is all that is known of her final hours. When she was found abandoned, her ship's boat was still on board, meaning her crew didn't leave the ship in their own vessel. She was stranded in about six feet of water on rocks. Somehow, she had escaped breaking up, and was not even leaking. The French authorities lightened the vessel by removing a hundred tons of coal and then towed her to Cherbourg.

In 1918, the *Zebrina* was fitted with auxiliary engine power and after being sold off by the Ajax shipping company was brought from Portchester to Milton.

THE MYSTERY IN A NUTSHELL...

As to her mysterious fate, the writer presented the reader with these options to consider:

• Enemy submarine or vessel boarded the schooner and did away with her crew.
• Enemy submarine took crew on deck and had to dive hurriedly.
• Enemy submarine took crew on board and below as prisoners, being eventually sunk.
• Swept off the schooner by heavy seas.
• Crew abandoned the schooner, thinking they were going down through heavy weather or on sighting a submarine or enemy vessel

To add to the mystery, the writer added:

In endeavouring to unravel the tangle and solve this knotty problem, old salts will remember that:

The ship's log, register, and boat were found on board.

No effects of the crew were ever received or traced.

The ship was found practically in an undamaged condition and the crew did not reach prison camps in Germany.

NOT HER FINAL RESTING PLACE...

The story didn't finish here. In June 1937, it was announced in the *Western Daily Press* that the ship was sold at auction for £50 to a local metal merchant. The report doesn't say whom, but I wonder if it was one of the Pounds family - the biggest scrap metal merchants in the town? (If you know, please tell us on the Mysteries of Portsmouth facebook group.)

The new owner then announced he was going to change the ship's name... to none other than *Mary Celeste*.

MURDERED WIFE

Another story of eerie goings-on at sea in the age of sail appeared in the *Hampshire Telegraph* on 19th May 1906. It told of a time in the 18th Century when Britain was at war with France and prize ships were brought back to Portsmouth. The story is expertly told:

THE GHOST OF THE MEDEE

In the year 1744 the *Dreadnought* man-of-war, under Captain Boscawen, cruising in the Channel, captured the French frigate Medee. A prize crew was put in her, and she was ordered to Portsmouth.

The first night on board there was a terrible hubbub amongst the French prisoners in the hold. They had seen a ghost, they declared, a ghost that had haunted the ship for the past three weeks. Their boatswain, the Frenchmen said, had three weeks ago murdered his wife, whom he had brought to sea with him, and though the man had been hanged, the woman's ghost still haunted the ship.

Before the Medee got to Spithead, some of the English prize crew swore that they had seen the ghost too.

The Medee, on arrival, was not thought good enough for the British Navy, and was sold to a privateer captain. He rechristened her the Boscawen, and sailed away in her to cruise in the Channel. But the crew had no luck. One morning an old sailor, the steadiest and soberest man in the ship, came to the quarterdeck and told the Captain that he had on the night before seen a ghost on board, which had told him that the ship was doomed to be lost.

Captain Walker—it was the famous Fortunatus Walker— reassured the men; but the tale soon spread, and after that other men said they saw the ghost, and the whole ship in the end became panic-stricken.

It was December, just before Christmas, in very wild and stormy weather. Now the ship, which had been badly built, began to leak like a sieve. Her head was turned for England, but it soon became more and more doubtful if she would ever reach there.

Again the ghost was seen, and shortly after that the men, panic-stricken anew, formed a design to seize the boats and make off, and trust to some passing ship to pick them up.

The plan was only stopped by the Captain's watchfulness. "With his pistols in his belt, he never quitted the quarter-deck nor once lay down for seven days, sleeping only as he stood, leaning on the barricade or rail of the quarter-deck, for the men watched every motion and every word, and had he disappeared a minute it is believed the duty of the ship had stopped, the officers themselves sometimes being as despondent as the men."

The ship managed at length, with extreme difficulty, to reach St. Ives, on the coast of Cornwall. She was by now too deep with the water in her hold to anchor in the roads, and boats had to be put off to tow her to the pier.

They failed to get command of her. A heavy sea drove the ship bodily on a reef, and as she touched she broke up.

The wreck was near enough the shore, however, for the crew to be saved by shore boats—all except three men;

those three were the very men who had sworn positively they had seen the ghost and had been spoken to by it.

It is a fabulous ghost story. So, was it based on true events? ...More research is required, and all theories are gratefully received!

THE ARCTIC SHIP THAT WOULD NOT GO

SHRIEKS FROM DEAD ESKIMO

The above was the headline of another fabulous spine chiller of a ghost story with a Portsmouth element, purporting to be true.

Published in the *Western Morning News* on 10th December 1934, here is the article in full:

(My old friend Mr. W. J. Grant has honoured me by a request to read through this true ghost story. The experience befell him many years ago, and I fully agree with him that it is well worth recording. —E. M. DELAFIELD.)

As most of the people mentioned in this story must be dead, I, the youngest of the party, being close on 81 years of age, there can be no harm in mentioning names when necessary.

In the year 1875, the Government fitted out two ships, the *Alert* and *Discovery*, Capt. A. H. Markham commanding the Alert and Capt. Stephenson the *Discovery*.

The *Pandora*, owned by Sir Allan Young, had been with McClintock in search of the remains of Sir John Franklin, and was most anxious to try to make the North-West Passage. However, the Government begged him first to try and communicate with and take letters to *Alert* and *Discovery*, which had sailed up Smith's Sound, on the West Coast of Greenland, with the hope of getting to the Pole that way. The Government gave Sir Allan £4,000.

Our ship, the *Pandora*, was nearly crushed by the ice in Melville Bay, and all boats were taken out on the ice and

well provisioned. Eventually the ship was saved, but we were quite unable to go further North owing to the heavy pack ice, and finally reached Disco, a Danish settlement, and here the ghost story begins.

HOME-WARD BOUND

As it was our last night in these parts, the Governor gave us a feast, and the men were given leave to be ashore. But our young doctor excused himself and did not go; he also kept back one man. Next day we set sail, homeward bound, in the direction of Cape Farewell, the most southern point of Greenland.

I was the official photographer on board, and performed other duties as well. My dark-room was a small place that used to be a store-room down in the engine-room, and at the end there was an iron ventilating shaft from the dark-room sticking up some eight inches from the deck.

It appears that a fireman named Griffith—we called him "Deaffy" because he was stone deaf—had left a chisel hammer in the engine-room, and he managed to open the hatchway to get his tools.

On returning forward he appeared to be in a very frightened state, and he told his messmates that he had heard a ghost in Mr. Grant's dark-room. They said, "Rubbish; ghosts did not make noises, and if they did, how could a deaf man hear them?"

We had on board a Dutch officer, Lieut. Koolemans Beynen, and every night I did my middle watch with him— that is from midnight to 4 a.m.

Our progress was slow, in fact, we did not seem to get on at all. Towards Cape Farewell, and in every direction we tried to sail, the wind always headed us.

WOMAN SHRIEKING

As Beynen and I were passing the ventilator into the dark-room one night we heard a woman's shriek coming through the ventilator. We both jumped aside, and Beynen said, "That must be Deaffy's ghost." At the end of our watch (4 a.m.) we told the duty relief officer, who happened to be the first lieutenant, about this, and he said we had better go down into the engine-room and see what it all meant.

We did not like the job, so it was put off till the morning.

Sir Allan then ordered Mr. Ball, the chief engineer, to go down with us and investigate. My dark-room was padlocked and all seemed secure. I opened the door, and there we saw a long box. This was brought on deck and opened, and was found to contain the body of a woman cut up, her legs and arms having been sawn off.

The funeral service was read and the body consigned to the deep. From that moment the wind shifted and blew from dead aft, and in a very short time we had passed Cape Farewell and soon arrived in Bantry Bay, Ireland.

Now the explanation of this was that an anthropological society in London, being anxious to secure bones of an Eskimo woman had given our young doctor £100 to obtain them. The doctor had noticed that a woman had lately been buried in the settlement. The Eskimos could not dig a grave in the solid rock, so they simply placed the coffin on the ground and covered it with a pile of stones.

The doctor, and the man with him therefore had no difficulty in taking the body when cut up to ship and placing it in a box marked Surgical Apparatus, his intention being to deliver it up to the anthropological society on the the arrival of the ship at Portsmouth.

A "TRUE" STORY..?

I find this story fascinating, not least because it appears to show that at some point in our illustrious past, grave-robbing was considered quite acceptable as a pastime for a man of science...

But then, isn't that essentially what Lord Carnarvon on his expedition to Egypt was doing in 1923? And wasn't it only that the original culture was long passed that made it acceptable? So, perhaps stories of curses around graves exist as part of our respect for the dead?

As for the matter of whether this story was true or not, once more further research is required.

Is it a well-delivered tale based on fact, or a work of pure fiction?

If only Mr Grant were available for further interview!

14
SEA MONSTERS
AND
SEA SERPENTS

OUT OF
THE DEPTHS

As well as stories of uncanny events occurring above the water, the question of what lies beneath has for millennia fired the imagination of sailors confronted with the vast and otherworldly nature of the lonely sea. Just so with legends of the sea monsters recounted to amazed listeners since the earliest times. The biblical story of the Leviathan tells the myth of a monster of the deep waiting to surface in time for the end of the world, while the legendary Scandinavian Kraken is a giant of the deeps the size of an island which feeds an entire ecosystem of fishes with its excrement. This is the reason why fisherman are attracted to its vicinity - but they had best be sharp about it if ever it decides to surface!

These gigantic creatures have their smaller relatives in sea serpents, and it's surprising how recently they have been reported by apparently reliable sources making their ways back to Portsmouth.

UNFATHOMABLE
MONSTER MYSTERY

A famous sea serpent sighting reported in the *Essex Standard* on 20th October 1848 tells of *HMS Daedalus*, a frigate under Captain McQuhae, which had arrived at Portsmouth on the 4th October. On the passage home, between the Cape of Good Hope and St Helena, the article states the Captain, and most of her officers and crew "saw a sea serpent that was 60 feet long on the surface with a further 40 feet below," and whose

83

jaws were "capacious to admit of a tall man standing upright between them."

The sighting caused a sensation, and the *Dover Telegraph and Cinque Ports General Advertiser* gave more details the following day, now placing the *Daedalus* at Plymouth, but also mentioning another sighting in recent months:

THE GREAT SEA SERPENT

The *Yankee* Captain's story of the great sea serpent having been kept in sight of his ship for five days, will scarcely be questioned, after the report of Captain M'Quhae, of Her Majesty's ship *Daedalus*. The Admiralty having

"Her Majesty's ship *Daedalus*, Hamoaze, Oct. 11, 1848.

"SIR - In reply to your letter of this day's date, requiring information as to the truth of a statement published of a sea serpent of extraordinary dimensions having been seen from Her Majesty's ship *Daedalus*, under my command, on her passage from the East Indies, I have the honour to acquaint you, for the information of my Lords of the Admiralty, that at five o'clock p.m. on the 6th Aug. last, in latitude 24 deg. 44 min. south, and longitude 9 deg. 22 min. east, the weather dark and cloudy, wind fresh from N. W., with a long ocean swell from the S. W., the ship on the port tack, heading N.E. by N., something very unusual was seen by Mr. Sartorius, Midshipman,

seen some accounts of this monster in the daily papers, called upon the Commander-in-Chief at Plymouth to request of Capt. M'Quhae to furnish a confirmation or denial of the statement, whereupon the gallant Captain immediately sent in the following report, which was officially transmitted to the Admiralty, and thence we have received the following most interesting and authentic copy. We may remark that it was the subject of great complaint at the Cape the *Daedalus* left, that some monster had recently visited Simon's-bay, and had driven away, or had consumed, all the fish. It is to be regretted that sufficient time was not afforded for an attempt to destroy the serpent with one or two discharges of grape shot:

rapidly approaching the ship from before the sea beam; the circumstance was immediately reported by him to the Officer of the watch, Lieutenant Edgar Drummond, with whom and Mr. Wm. Barrett, the Master, I was at the time walking the quarter-deck. The ship's company were at supper.

"On our attention being called to the object it was discovered to be an enormous serpent, with head and shoulders kept about four feet constantly above the surface of the sea, and as nearly as we could approximate, by comparing it with the length of what our maintopsail yard would show in the water, there was at the very least 60 feet of the animal, 'a Fleur d'eau,' no portion of which was to our perception used in propelling it through the water either by vertical or horizontal undulation. It passed rapidly, but so close under our lee quarter, that had it been a man of my acquaintance I should have easily recognised his features with the naked eye; and it did not, either in approaching the ship, or after it had passed our wake, deviate in the slightest degree from its course to the south-west, which it held on at the pace of from 12 to 15 miles an hour, apparently on some determined purpose.

"The diameter of the serpent was about 15 or 16 inches behind the head, which was, without any doubt, that of a snake, and never, during the twenty minutes that it continued in sight of our glasses, once below the surface of the water. Its colour a dark brown, with yellowish white about the throat. It had no fins, but something like the mane of a horse, or rather a bunch of seaweed washed about its back. It was seen by the Quartermaster, the Boatswain, Mate, and the man at the wheel, in addition to myself and Officers above mentioned.

"I am having a drawing of this serpent made from a sketch taken immediately after it was seen, which I hope to have ready for transmission to my Lords Commissioners of the Admiralty by to-morrow's post.

"I have the honor to be, Sir, your most obedient humble servant,

"P. M'QUHAE, Captain.
"Admiral Sir W. Gage, &c., Devonport."

JAW-DROPPING SIZE

While the earlier report described the sea serpent's jaws as wide enough to "admit a tall man standing", this more sober letter from a Royal Naval officer put the creature's body at 16 inches - that is, about 40cm. It is possible the creature had extremely long and flexible jaws to enable the aforementioned tall man enough headroom, but there is no doubt that news improves once the facts are out of the way.

Another such serpent had a more illustrious witness. An article in the *Portsmouth Times* reported that Commander Hugo L. Pearson, of the *Osborne* Royal Yacht, newly arrived at Portsmouth had forwarded to the Admiralty another sighting of a sea monster the yacht encountered during her homeward voyage. The sighting was summarised in the *Gloucester Citizen* on 13th June 1877:

The report states that about five o'clock on the afternoon of the 2nd instant, while the yacht was proceeding round the north coast of Sicily towards Cape Vito, the officer on watch observed a long ridge of fins, each about six feet long, moving slowly along, the sea being very calm at the time. He called for a telescope, and was at once joined by other officers. The *Osborne* was steaming westward at a speed of about 10 knots an hour, and the fins were progressing in an eastwardly direction. As the yacht met the fins those on board noticed the foremost part of a gigantic sea monster. Its skin was apparently devoid of scales, and was almost as sleek as a seal. The head was bullet-shaped, with an elongated termination, being somewhat like that of a seal, and about six feet diameter. Its features were only seen by one officer, who described them as like those of an alligator. The neck appeared to be narrow and the body was somewhat like that of a turtle, a fin about 15 feet long extending from either side. The appearance of the monster is accounted for by a submarine volcano which occurred north of Galita, in the Gulf of Sunice, about the middle of May. The spot in question is about 104 miles distant from where the monster is reported to have been seen.

The news was recycled by the *Irish Times* and *Dundee Courier* among many others in the following days, until the sighting entered into the public psyche as settled fact.

SCALES AND SCEPTICS

One reporter in the *Leeds Times* on 16th June 1877, however, took a far more sceptical attitude, as this ironic report reveals:

The Sea-serpent Again.—According to the *Portsmouth Times* the sea-serpent has lately turned up in the Mediterranean, on the north coast of Sicily, near Cape Vito; and, to make assurance doubly sure, the ship from which he was descried was the royal yacht *Osborne*, Commander H. L. Pearson, which has just put into Portsmouth Harbour. Despatches, it is stated, have been forwarded by the commander of the *Osborne* to the Admiralty setting forth how, about two p.m. on the 2nd inst., the sea being exceptionally calm, the officer of the watch observed "a long ridge of fins, each about six feet in length, moving slowly along."

He called for a telescope, and was at once joined by other officers. The fins seemed to be progressing in an easterly direction, and as the *Osborne* came nearer "they were replaced by the foremost part of gigantic sea monster, its skin devoid of scales, and altogether as sleek as a seal."

Its head was bullet-shaped, with "elongated termination," and was about six feet in diameter. Its features were only seen by one officer, who described them as being "like those of an alligator;" but this may be only so much of the sea-serpent's artfulness.

The monster has shown, ever since good Bishop Pontoppidan's time, that he can be all things to all men. He is the Proteus of the ocean; and, while he displays a seal-like head to one gallant mariner and alligator's countenance to another, it would not the least surprise us to learn that to a third observer he had looked like a whale—very like a whale.

When Captain M'Quhae, R.N., met him about a quarter of a century since, the serpent, if we remember aright, wore his hair long and floating over his abandoned dorsal vertebrae; but to the judicious observers on board the *Osborne* he appeared to be smooth-polled. Perhaps the sea-serpent is going bald or, it may be, has given all his mane away in love-locks to the mermaids.

At all events, the officers of the *Osborne* came, so it is said, to the conclusion that his neck was narrow, and that his body was developed in the form of a colossal turtle, having two fins, each about fifteen feet in length, by means of which he paddled himself along. Then the description of the interesting prodigy comes to sudden termination, as we are told that "the *Osborne* was steaming westward at the rate of ten and a half knots an hour, and, having a long passage before her, could not stay to make further observations."

It is, however, conjectured that the serpent has been violently projected from the bottom to the top of the sea by the eruption of "a submarine volcano," which eruption occurred in the Gulf of Tunis about the middle of last May. Another hypothesis might be warrantable, to the effect that the sea snake has been so intolerably annoyed of late by the laying down of torpedoes— dangerous things and not good to eat—in the Black Sea and the Danube, that he has given up the seafaring line of business in disgust, and, when the *Osborne* passed him, was leisurely paddling his way to the south coast of England, with a view to seeking an engagement at the Brighton Aquarium. Whether he is the old serpent that Captain M'Quhae saw, or a new snake, is uncertain; but on the whole he might well be our familiar acquaintance, for it cannot be denied that the story told about him has a very ancient and fishlike smell.

A NATURALIST'S OPINION

The scepticism of the journalist, however, was balanced by the open-mindedness of a naturalist interviewed by *The Times* and reported in the *Cumberland & Westmorland Herald* on 23rd June 1877, who took a more scientific approach to the question:

With reference to the above, Mr. Andrew Wilson, lecturer in Zoology and Comparative Anatomy at the Edinburgh Medical School, writes as follows in the *Times*: "About a year ago I ventilated in the columns of several journals the idea that the 'sea serpents' so frequently seen, were in reality giant tape fishes or riband fishes. While not meaning by this statement to exclude the idea that other animals—such as giant sea snakes themselves— may occasionally personate the 'sea serpent,' I am, as a zoologist, fully convinced that very many of the reported appearances of sea serpents are explicable on the supposition that giant tape fishes—of the existence of which no reasonable doubt can be entertained—have been seen.

The report of Captain Pearson, of the Royal Yacht *Osborne*, appears, as far as zoological characters are concerned, to be fully explained on the 'riband fish' theory. The long back fins, the scaleless skin, the rounded head, and, lastly, the two great side (or pectoral) fins, each measuring many feet in length, all form so many details corresponding exactly to the appearance of a great tape fish. I offer these observations with the view of showing that, given a recital founded, as I believe the present narrative to be, on fact, we possess in the lists of living and of well-known animals adequate representatives of the 'great unknown.'

THE GREAT UNKNOWN - AGAIN!

Inspired by these reports, a talk was given on the Sea Serpent for the Portsmouth Literary and Scientific Society the following year. The *Hampshire Telegraph* reported that on Saturday 23rd November 1878 "a paper on 'Sea Serpents' was read by Mr. Arthur Byng, the subject being illustrated by numerous diagrams."

Mr Byng's talk was titled *The Great Unknown*, although he said that it was claimed "to be partially known by some people". He related facts from "men of known capacity and repute," to try to fathom the reality of sea serpents. Modern knowledge, Mr. Byng stated, brought the inquirer after truth "far into the labyrinth of the vast, the wild, the terrible," adding that "remnants of bygone monsters" that once inhabited the globe "might still do so", for all they knew.

As for the species of the creature that was widely called a "sea serpent", Mr Byng was not willing to conjecture on its species. Mr Byng's talk told how:

The animal had been repeatedly seen on the coast of Norway. Five British officers saw it off Sambro, in 1831, Captain McQuhae and his officers saw it from the *Daedalus* in 1848, Captain Beechy saw it from the *Blossom*, Mr. Morris Sterling saw it in a Norwegian fjord, Mr. Davidson saw it from the *Royal Saxon* in 1829, Captain Steele and others saw it from the *Barham* in 1852 and Captain Harrington and his officers saw it from the *Castilian* in 1857. Nearly all the descriptions tallied with that of Captain McQuhae, who said that the head appeared four feet out of the water, and about 60 feet of its body in straight line on the surface, and that there must have been 30 feet or 40 feet more under the water, by which it propelled itself at the rate of 15 miles an hour. The diameter of the

However, Byng added that "a master of science", Professor Richard Owen "gave his verdict against the serpentine character of the animal, and pronounced it in his judgment, to have been a seal or a sea elephant."

AN UNDISCOVERED SPECIES?

So, what was it?

Mr Byng wondered whether it could be an entirely unrecorded species, and he gave his own experience while on a voyage to Jamaica when "the ship was surrounded continuously for 17 hours with a troop of whales of a species which was certainly undescribed." Byng claimed to have had ample opportunity for examination, and though it was not a sea serpent, what he saw "was a whale of large size occurring in great numbers in the North Atlantic, which on no other occasion had fallen under scientific observation."

He argued: "Were not those facts, then, sufficiently weighty to restrain them from rejecting so great an amount of testimony to the so-called sea serpent merely on the ground that its dead remains had not come under examination?"

exposed part of the body was about 18 inches, and when it extended its jaws, which were full of large jagged teeth, they seemed sufficiently capacious to admit of a tall man standing upright between them.

Mr Byng had taken the original newspaper report at its word regarding the size of the jaws, which McQuhae's letter to the Admiralty reproduced above did not confirm. How easily *alternative facts* slip into the consciousness!

He added that confirmation of the creature reported by Captain McQuhae was given "immediately by an eminent nobleman who had long resided on the coast of Norway, and he gave confirmatory evidence of the existence of the animal on that coast."

In conclusion, Byng expressed his own confident persuasion that there existed some oceanic animal of immense proportions which had not yet been received into the category of scientific zoology.

WIT OF FOOLS

In his reply to the talk, the Rev J Knapp was an enthusiast for the sea serpent, asking: "What did they know of the contents of the mighty depths? If they visited the aquaria - and he believed he had seen the largest of them in Europe - they encountered a great variety of fish of which they knew little or nothing, and, therefore, on that account they ought not to reject the subject which had that evening so ably been brought under their notice." He finished with the observation that "incredulity" was "the wit of fools."

CHASING THE SPITHEAD SEA-SERPENT

A later sighting by Vice-Admiral Gore Jones, however, might incline the seeker-after-truth to call those who chose to believe in sea monsters the fools. Gore-Jones related his experience in the *Willesden Chronicle* of 26th October 1883:

"In 1848 I was attached to her Majesty's ship *St. Vincent*, bearing the flag of Sir Charles Napier, and laying at Spithead. One summer evening, about six o'clock. just as the officers were sitting down to dinner, the midshipman of the watch ran into the wardroom and reported that a sea serpent was passing rapidly between the ship and the Isle of Wight (this was after the reported appearance of the *Daedalus* sea serpent).

All got our glasses and went on deck, and there, sure enough, about a mile off, was a large monster, with a head and shaggy mane, about 100 feet long, and tapering towards the tail; it was going with the tide, and had a rapid, undulating motion. Two or three boats were manned, and some officers got their guns and went in pursuit. We watched them from the ship; they gradually got close, and guns were raised and levelled at the creature's head ; but just as we thought the sport was about to begin, down went the guns, and from their gestures we saw something very laughable had occurred.

On their return we found that the supposed serpent was a long line of soot. Some steamer in the Southampton waters had evidently swept her dirty flues, and the soot from tubes or flues is always of very sticky nature, and as it was pitched overboard it went away with the tide, sticking together, and gradually forming into the shape of a long serpent, the wave motion giving it an undulating life-like appearance. In this case, if the boats had not gone we should have all believed we had seen the real sea serpent."

Despite this contrary evidence for sea serpents, even the Vice-Admiral acknowledged the existence of a "real sea serpent" - and they continued to be seen in far flung parts of the world and reported on their return to Portsmouth.

The Nottingham Evening Post of 31st May 1899 told how the crew of *HMS Narcissus*, recently returned to Portsmouth from the China Station sighted just such a sea creature on her homeward voyage. In the ship's log dated May 21st ran the entry: "Observed sea monster on port bow, certainly over 150 feet in length."

Of other sea monsters, there is an intriguing account in the *Portsmouth Evening News* for 11th January 1929, which simply states:

SEA MONSTERS

There is exhibited in the PictureHouse,Commercial Road, an extraordinary collection of sea monsters: Mermaids which were captured recently from the Red Sea. They have head, eyes, nose, tongue, chin, hands, fingers, and a fish-like tail.

It all sounds intriguing... Yet, the mystery is explained by another article that appeared in the *Hampshire Telegraph* in August 1903 written by the famous expert in mythological creatures, S Baring-Gould:

As for the mermaids exhibited in shows at fairs, very beautiful according to the painted canvas without, very ugly when seen within, they are manufactured articles, made in Japan, out of the upper portion of a monkey, most ingeniously grafted on to a spotted tail of a fish, so ingeniously indeed that it is most difficult to distinguish the junction.

Though these mermaids were of exotic origin, Mr Baring-Gould had not read another article in the *Hampshire Telegraph* that revealed a "man who makes monsters" lived much closer to home in Lambeth. The article confided:

The taxidermist in question is wonderfully ingenious, and he cures, stuffs and joins together parts of half a dozen different creatures so as to produce a veritable monster that will astonish country folks. His whole life is spent at this business.

Not all monster mysteries could be so easily explained away, however. Yet another sea serpent raised its head at Spithead before World War 2, which the *Portsmouth Evening News* reported with glee on 24th May 1938:

A SEA MONSTER! PORTSMOUTH ANGLER SEES ONE AT SPITHEAD

Southsea is at last coming into line with other popular seaside resorts, such as Loch Ness. Monsters have been the vogue for years in Scotland, and a merman was seen off the Irish Coast by some fishermen last summer; but the South Coast has rather lagged behind in this respect. But now, the summer sea serpent's season having opened, Portsmouth is well in the forefront with a five-humped 35-foot monster! Mr. William Oastler, who is engineer at the Gordon Sanitary Laundry, saw it.

He was fishing with some friends two miles off the Spit Buoy, when he was suddenly confronted with this latest addition to the monster history of the South Coast. In an interview, he said:—"It was a funny looking object, with about four or five humps and about 35 feet long. We were anchored when I first saw it, and it was a bit windy, I am not a very good swimmer, and did not know what might happen if it got under the boat, but it was heading fast for the Isle of Wight." Mr. Oastler and his two friends had seen sufficient of porpoises to be certain they were not confusing this monster with them. He described it as being a silvery grey colour, with its humps standing four or five feet out of the water.

Yet another sea monster was reported by the *Hampshire Telegraph* on 10th December 1943:

A BRITISH submarine's encounter with an unidentified sea monster is described by the British Information Services, whose source is an official report made by the vessel's commander. Lt. D. V. Campbell. Just before surfacing one evening the crew hit a slight thud, and it was discovered later that the voice pipe and open sights on the deck had been flattened and much paint had been scraped away from the deck gun, which was covered with black slime, giving off an "exceedingly ancient and fish-like smell."

Was that final line deliberately ironic? If not, it appears that not even the turmoil of war was enough to deter sea serpents from appearing! The only question left to ask is:
Were any of these sightings real..?

15
SOME
COUNTRY GHOSTS

A HAUNTED
LANDSCAPE?

Away from the Navy and out of town, the villages and country estates around Portsmouth and deeper into Hampshire also have their own legends, myths and ghost stories.

Near the coast, in eerie, dark and dismal spots, the wild coastline was full of unexpected movement in reeds and bushes, sudden splashes, the cries of night-time birds and animals. Here, smugglers plied their illicit trade, prowling the deserted creeks and inlets. Ever seeking to cloak their activities from the eyes of the landguard and coastguard,

they might well have encouraged or even created stories of hauntings, ghosts and evil spirits to keep superstitious locals away, and this may account for many a ghostly tale.

That said, it's also true that smugglers' yarns don't explain every ghost sighting.

Just so with this wonderful tale of an apparition at Warblington, reprinted in the *Hampshire Telegraph* of 26th December 1919.

The original long report was written in 1695 by a curate named Wilkins, based in Havant. It is a detailed, spine-tingling account, which I think you'll agree is worthy of being reprinted in full:

THE WARBLINGTON GHOST
A LOCAL LEGEND

The following singular, and apparently authentic narrative is contained in a letter written by Caswell, the mathematician, to the celebrated Dr. Bentley. He says he he wrote it down from the lips of the principal actor, who was Curate of Warblington, near Portsmouth, and B.A. of Trinity College, Oxford, and who would swear to tell the truth of it as far as he was concerned.

December 11th, 1695.

At Warblington, near Havant, in Hampshire, within six miles of Portsmouth, in the Parsonage house dwelt Thomas Pierce, the tenant, with his wife and child, a man servant, Thomas, and a maid servant.

About the beginning of August, 1695, on a Monday, about 9 or 10 at night, all being gone to bed, except the maid with the child; the maid being in the kitchen, and having raked up the fire, took a candle in one hand, and the child in the other arm and turning about saw a man in a black gown walking through the room and thence out of the door into the orchard. Upon, this the maid hasting upstairs cried out, upon which the master and mistress ran down, and found her with the candle in her hand and grasping the child about the neck with the other arm. She told them the reason of her crying out, and would not that night tarry in the house, but removed to another, belonging to Henry Salter, farmer; where she cried out all the night from the terror she was in, and she could not be persuaded to go any more to the house upon any terms.

On the morrow (i.e., Tuesday) the tenant's wife came to me, lodging then at Havant, to desire my advice, and consult with some friends about it. I told her I thought it was a flam [i.e. a hoax - ed], and that they had a mind to abuse Mr. Brereton, the Rector, whose house it was; she desired me to come up; I told her I would come up, and sit up or lie there, as she pleased, for then as to all stories of ghosts and apparitions, I was an infidel.

I went thither and sat up the Tuesday night, with the tenant and his man-servant. About twelve or one o'clock I searched all the rooms in the house to see if anybody were hid there to impose upon me. At last we came into a lumber room, and there I smiling, told the tenant that was with me that I would call for the apparition, if there was any, and oblige him to come. The tenant seemed to be afraid, but I told him that I would defend him from harm, and then I repeated "Barbara celerant Darii, etc.," jestingly. [These obscure words from philosophy have nothing to do with protection against spirits - ed]

At this the tenant's countenance changed, so that he was ready to drop down with fear. When I told him I perceived he was afraid, and I would prevent its coming, and repeated "Baralipton," etc., [more meaningless words] then he recovered his spirits pretty well, and we

left the room and went down into the kitchen, and sat up there the remaining part of the night, and had no manner of disturbance.

Thursday night the tenant and I lay together in one room and the man in another room, and he saw something walk along in a black gown and place itself against a window. It there stood for some time and then walked off.

Friday morning the man relating this, I asked him why he did not call me, and I told him I thought it was a trick or a flam; he told me the reason why he did not call me was that he was not able to speak or move for dread.

Friday night we lay as before, and Saturday night, and had no disturbance either of the nights.

Sunday night I lay by myself in one room, not that where the man saw the apparition, and the tenant and his man in one bed in another room; and betwixt twelve and two the man heard something walk in their room at the bed's foot, and whistling at last it came to the bed's side, drew the curtain and looked on them, after some time it moved off; then the man railed to me, and desired me to come, for that there was something in the room that went about whistling. I asked him whether he had any light, or could strike one, he told me no; then I leaped out of bed, and not staying to put on my clothes, went out of my room and along a gallery to the door, which I found locked or bolted.

I desired them to unlock the door for I could not get in; he then got out of bed and opened the door, which was near, and went immediately to bed again. I went out in three or four steps, and it being a moonlight night I saw the apparition move from the bed side, and clap up against the wall that divided their room and mine.

I went and stood directly against it within my arms length of it, and asked it in the name of God, what it was that made it come disturbing of us. I stood some time expecting an answer, and receiving none, thinking it might be some fellow hid in the room to frighten me, I put out my arm to feel it, and my hand seemingly went through the body of it, and felt no manner of substance till it came to the wall; then I drew back my hand, and still it was in the same place.

Till now I had not the least fear, and even now had very little; then I adjured it to tell me what it was. When I had said those words, it, keeping its back against the wall moved gently along toward the door. I followed it, and it going out at the door, turned its back towards me and went along the gallery. I followed it a little into the gallery, and it disappeared, where there was no corner for it to turn, and before it came to the end of the gallery where was the stairs. Then I found myself very cold, from my feet as high as my middle, though I was not in great fear.

I went into the bed betwixt the tenant and his man, and they complained of my being exceedingly cold. The man leaned over his master in the bed, and saw me stretch out my hand toward the apparition, and heard me speak the words, the tenant also heard the words.

The apparition seemed to have a morning gown of a darkish colour, no hat nor cap, short black hair, a thin, meagre visage, of a pale colour, seemed to be about forty-five to fifty years old; the eyes half shut, the arms hanging down; the hands visible beneath the sleeve; of a middle stature. I related this description to Mr. John Lardner, rector of Havant, and to Major Battin, of Langstone, in Havant Parish, and they both said the description agreed very well to Mr. P—, a former rector of the place, who has been dead above twenty years.

Upon this the tenant and his wife left the house, which has remained void since. The Monday after last Michaelmas day, a man having been at Havant Fair passed by the fore-said parsonage house about nine or ten at night and saw a light in most of the rooms 0f the house; he, wondering at the sight, looked into the kitchen window, and saw only a light, but turning himself to go away he saw the appearance of a man in a long gown; he made haste away, and the apparition followed him over a piece of glebe land of several acres, to a lane which he crossed, over a little meadow, then over another lane to some pales, which belong to Henry Salter, my landlord, near a barn, in which were several of the farmer's men.

The man went into the barn, and told them how he was frightened and followed from the parsonage house by an apparition, which they might see standing against the pales, if they went out; they went out, and saw it scratch against the pales, and make hideous noise, it stood there some time, and then disappeared; their description agreed with what I saw.

This account I had from the man himself, whom it followed, and also from the farmer's men.

THOMAS WILKINS. Curate of Warblington.

Mr Brereton, the Rector, would have nothing said of the story, for that he can get no tenant, though he has offered the house for ten pounds a year less. Mr. P— the former incumbent, whom the apparition represented was a man of very ill report. Those who know this P— say that he had exactly such a gown and that he used to whistle. I desire you not to suffer any copy of this to be taken, lest an unwanted bookseller should print it.

(I should add to this final note from the original author, that as a bookseller I hope I am not *entirely* unwanted!)

FARLINGTON MARSHES

Another desolate area on the coast not far from Warblington is the marshland and few dwindling fields of Farlington.

These days, the former village of Farlington has become a suburb of Portsmouth, and Farlington's much reduced marshes exist as part of a Nature Reserve.

On 14th March 1930, the *Hampshire Telegraph* printed a long article about the Black House that used to stand here, and which had an eerie reputation. Here, once again, the surroundings were part of the whole picture that made the place so otherworldly. The article, entitled *The Black House*, began:

Within a few miles of Portsmouth and almost within hearing of the roar of the trains and of the ever-increasing road traffic, there stands a building which has weathered the storms of over a century and has a history which is a locked and tantalizing secret. It is the old Black House, which appears in bold relief against the blue of the sea, just off Farlington Marshes.

Its name is derived, perhaps, from its forbidding colour, for the walls are tarred to preserve them from the inclemencies of the weather; or maybe it owes its title to the somewhat sinister reputation it has gained amongst the few old fisher folk who still linger along the neighbouring coastline as reminders of one of Portsmouth's waning industries.

Built on an artificial island, connected to the mainland by a slippery causeway and surrounded by boulders which act as a breakwater, the Black House presents a stern and sturdy front to even the wildest weather. Indeed according to the present owner, Mr. Russell, of the little village of Langstone, in whose family the building has been so long, those terrific gales which swept the British Isles in the first week of December last, and again on the night of January 12, only loosened a few odd tiles from the venerable red roof. The house cannot but arouse the curiosity of any who may see it and who, standing in silent contemplation, hear the wild cries of the plover and the gulls, and the soft, continuous hissing of water sucking through muddy ooze. The very inaccessibility of the building lends enchantment to the view, for unless one takes a boat, which means a row of an hour or so, one has to go overland, along the ruinous sea wall which skirts the Marshes...

Thus, the piece's moody introduction to the now long-demolished Black House. But, was it *really* haunted, or did it just give the writer the "creeps"? It seems it didn't take much for a solitary location to do that to this journalist. All that was needed was for it to be isolated, difficult to approach, and old enough for people not to be able to remember when it was built.

Though the article was long on mood, it was short on detail and event. The writer clearly enjoyed the *possibility* of some kind of ghostly presence there, and revelled in its unknown history, filling the column inches with unfounded hints and rumours. Indeed, he later asserted:

THE GHOST AND THE SKELETON

Like all old buildings, especially those which have connexions with the seafaring trade, the Black House is haunted. That this should be its reputation is not at all surprising, for the coast, which is almost as wild now as it was in the early half of the last century, has seen many stirring encounters between smugglers and Excisemen.

In fact, not so very long ago a skeleton was unearthed on one of the innumerable small "binnaces," or islands, abounding in Emsworth Harbour; and who knows but that it was the bony framework of some unfortunate smuggler who fell foul of the Customs officers? Does his uneasy spirit still haunt the scenes where he used to run with his laces and wines before they were hidden in the deep cellars which to this day undermine the houses of the flourishing town of Emsworth?

We see with this article one of the real problems for the seeker of ghost stories. The writer has fixed in his mind that there *must* be a ghost story connected to the site, and tries hard to convince us of it, too. Yet he offers no history or events to support his assertion.

It's a great example of what happens when the imagination runs away with a journalist's pen.

The article shows us in a clear way how a creepy feeling, a strong desire for a romantic story and a few unanswered questions can start up the rumour mill that lies at the heart of so many, but not all, ghost stories...

THE MILLAND MONK

This was not the only time a journalist argued too hard for a ghostly presence. Another such "ghost" was reported by the *Portsmouth Evening News* on 24th January 1933 at Milland church, which is about 7 miles north-east of Petersfield. The report stated a ghost had been seen by a resident, although it hastened to add that most locals didn't believe it:

The chapel, which from the reign of Edward VI was the only place of worship in the neighbourhood for 300 years, used to be closely associated with a near-by monastery, and the witness of the supposed phantom declares that it was in the form of an evil monk with an expression on his face of intense rage.

From inquiries made in the district, I have discovered that an apparition similar to the one reputed to have been seen recently is said to have shown itself near the old chapel many years ago. The story is that the ghost appeared to bar the way, as though trying to prevent worshippers from entering the building; and those who believe in the existence of the spectre regard it as significant that the chapel is never used for evening services.

The report explained that a newer chapel was built near the old one, and being easier to heat and light, and much more comfortable, this one was used for evening services.

Rather than a response to a haunting, the use of the newer chapel simply appeared to be a better choice... but the writer persisted, describing the "eerie atmosphere" of the older chapel and churchyard, and assuring readers of a belief among some "that if any evening services were to be held in the chapel, the phantom monk would again be seen."

Little explanation was given for the appearance of this monk, except an assertion that "the apparition is a link with far-off days before the dissolution of the Monasteries."

The writer continued looking for a story - but it was as elusive as the ghost itself and resorted to mood pictures:

Anyone visiting the magnificent old churchyard in the gathering dusk might well be excused for believing that there is some truth in the ghost story...

I must confess that I was deeply impressed by the atmosphere that surrounds the historical building. It may have been because of the great age of the ivy-covered walls; possibly it was caused by the proximity of the mossy graves which lie in rows beneath the brooding trees, or perhaps I was affected by the intense quietness around me in a churchyard well-known for its beauty.

Whatever the cause, there is to my mind something which I shall call unusual about the atmosphere around Milland Chapel as compared with other country churchyards which I have visited; something which makes it easy to believe the legend that a ghost has been seen seated on the well-worn steps leading to the gallery where the choir were wont to sing in the olden days...

And so the article went on in the same vein...

SECRET TUNNEL

With many myths about ancient buildings it is often the case that secret passageways are part of the mix, and the Milland Monk report mentioned the possibility of a tunnel supposedly linking the chapel to the demolished monastery that once stood at Milland Place. The writer then asked: "Can you wonder that there is a ghost story at Milland?"

To this, I have to answer, "No, not with you trying so hard to make one!" The article finished:

I first heard of the legend connected with the picturesque part of the Portsmouth Road from a gentleman holding a prominent position in the parish. His comment was: "It is quite possible that anyone who is sensitive to such things may have seen a phenomenon of the kind, although I have not seen it myself and very few of the parishioners are interested in the story. In spite of this I have no real reason for doubting that it actually appeared at some time or other." He added that the person who was supposed to have seen the apparition was terrified and ran out of the churchyard.

So, despite all the writer's obvious efforts to create a ghostly atmosphere, is there a ghost? If you are so minded, perhaps the chapel is worth a visit to find out for yourself!

A CHALTON APPARITION

From an ancient chapel where the writer longed for ghosts, to a story of a hardheaded man who meets an apparition in the wilds of Hampshire, with unexpected results. In this case, the story from the *Tavistock Gazette* on 3rd September 1858 tells of a bizarre real encounter at Chalton, near Butser on the London Road:

About this time two years, a friend of mine residing near Portsmouth, paid me a visit for a few days. He started for home about three o'clock on a Monday morning, as he wished to be early home, and had to walk the greater part of the way. I went with him for a distance of three miles or so, and I think I never saw so many meteors in the same time in my life as I did round the foot of Butser Hill. They seemed flitting about in all directions. About half an hour after my friend and I parted company, he took the footpath across a part of Chalton Down, as it was a little nearer and much pleasanter walking. The morning was very close and sultry, with a few low clouds sometimes driving along, and at other times resting on the tops of the hills, something like a thin fog, and there was beautiful moonlight. The attention of my friend was suddenly aroused by an enormous ghost, of most gigantic dimensions, who seemed in the shape off a human being, but in size almost incredible, and the worst of it was, Mr Ghost seemed to be striding furlongs at every step in his hurry to meet him. My friend stood, so did Mr Ghost. After a little consideration, the former, being a fine athletic young man, and one not easily frightened, resolved to examine Mr Ghost at closer quarters.

He therefore proceeded cautiously to meet his seemingly anxious-to-be companion. Mr Ghost seemed quite to anticipate his wish, and he likewise proceeded to meet the intruder upon his domain. Ghost seemed to be diminishing in size, and upon a nearer approach, a doubt began to arise in my friend's mind as to his intentions, and in order to anticipate any violence, he grasped his stick tightly in his hand and raised it up, so as to be ready for any emergency; ghost did the same.

My friend suddenly called to mind the "Spectre of the Brocken", and soon the whole mystery was solved. He actually counted the buttons on the spectre's vest, and saw every part of his own image clearly reflected by the light of the moon from one of the clouds moving slowly along the side of the hill. The story, which is a fact no less wonderful than true, is of some importance, and, possibly, some of your readers may have seen something similar in their day.

Though there is journalistic license in the story, the phenomenon it describes is real. A *Brocken spectre* is the observer's shadow cast on clouds by the sun or moon, magnified by a trick of the light to enormous proportions.

Where the story gains in the telling is from all that detail in the shadow. You cannot count the buttons on a shadow's vest! But overall, this apparition was genuine, for sure!

A TOMBSTONE CURSE DEFIED

Not all encounters in the countryside were so harmless. On 24th September 1786 a sailor bought food and drinks for three men at the Red Lion, Thursley, while heading to his ship in Portsmouth. The men followed him and murdered him on the rim of the Devil's Punch Bowl, Hindhead. In the savage attack they nearly severed his head from his body, then then threw his naked corpse into the Punch Bowl.

The men were apprehended at the Sun Inn in Rake, after trying to sell the dead man's clothes. They were tried and hanged from a triple gibbet at Gibbet Hill, a sight long associated in folk memory with the uncanny, it being rumoured to once have been a sight of pagan worship.

A stone was erected in memory of the grisly deed and the site was well enough known for Dickens to mention it in his novel *Nicholas Nickleby*, in which Nicholas relates the tale to Smike as they pass the desolate spot.

The stone, still standing, bears the following inscription:

ERECTED
In detestation of a barbarous Murder,
Committed on an unknown Sailor,

On Sep, 24th 1786,
By Edwd. Lonegon, Mich. Casey & Jas. Marshall.
Who were all taken the same day,
And hung in Chains near this place,
Whoso sheddeth Man's Blood,
by Man shall his Blood be shed.
Gen Chap 9 Ver 6

The unknown sailor was buried in Thursley churchyard, and it was rumoured that a curse would fall on anyone who moved the stone.

Even into the modern day, old stories of curses still have echoes, as this report from the *Daily Herald* on 10th December 1929 shows:

Navvies engaged in making a footpath by the side of the road which skirts the Devil's Punch Bowl, on the heights Hindhead, Surrey, have decided to draw lots to decide who will remove the tombstone of a sailor murdered on that spot many years ago, when the Portsmouth road in this district was the haunt of highwaymen.

On the back of the stone is a line placing a curse on anyone who moves it.

This has not upset the navvies in the least. "The idea of drawing lots was suggested as a joke," one of the highway officials assured a reporter. "Such things like that don't upset navvies. They would move anything curses or no curses."
The stone will still be a pilgrimage for the curious: for it is only to be set back a foot or two.

This story is reported as just a bit of fun on the navvies' part...

But you have to ask... if they didn't believe, then *why exactly* did they draw lots..?

THE CURSE OF NETLEY ABBEY

Another ancient site connected with a curse is Netley Abbey, a ruin which stands in the Royal Victoria Country Park near Southampton Water.

The Abbey was closed by the tyrant Henry VIII during the Dissolution of the Monasteries, that ruthless seizure of the Catholic Church's assets that came in the guise of religious reform.

A curse on the despoilers of the monasteries was reported by The *Portsmouth Evening News* on 19th June 1930, as follows:

COINCIDENCE OR JUDGMENT?

It may be a coincidence or a judgment, according to the point of view you adopt; but it is a remarkable fact that the curse of failure of male issue afflicted nearly all of the families that took part in the spoliation of the monasteries in the 16th Century. In all, 630 families are known to have shared the booty, and of them, 14 only have not been extinguished by failure of their male issues.

The article mentions one more strange event - that of a Southampton builder named Walter Taylor, who purchased the stonework of the church in 1700 for building purposes. The story goes that he was warned in a dream not to destroy the building. Sure enough, the West Window fell in and killed him... So, the site of a *real* curse then..?

A HAMPSHIRE GHOST STORY

As we near the end of this book, I have room for one more ghost story. I have saved a well-documented and baffling one for last. The remarkable tale of the Haunted Manor of Hinton Ampner, a small village around 20 miles north of Portsmouth in the South Downs is so well supported by witnesses that even though it happened a long way from Portsmouth, and its connection with the town is only through a naval officer residing nearby, it is well worth retelling.

I first encountered this story in the *Bristol Mercury* which held an extract from the full report that first appeared in issues of *The Gentleman's Magazine* in November and December 1872.

I reprint much of the story, since it is a fascinating account.

The full article is accompanied by supporting letters from witnesses who were servants, relatives and friends of Mary Ricketts, the writer of this long account of a haunting, which occurred after her family arrived there in 1765.

THE HAUNTING AT HINTON AMPNER

Mary Ricketts was the wife of William Ricketts, a wealthy plantation owner with estates in Jamaica. When he left Britain to tend his estate, Mary Ricketts chose to stay in England and look after her children, and the family moved into the manor house at Hinton Ampner. Many strange events occurred during their stay, and Mary had the presence of mind to write them down and gather witness statements, as well as drawing together all the ecorrespondence about the haunting. The full account can be found in *The Gentleman's Magazine* as mentioned above, but here is her own story extracted from the many accounts collected:

To my dear children I address the following relation, anxious that the truths which I so faithfully have delivered shall be as faithfully transmitted to posterity, to my own in particular. I determined to commit them to writing, which I recommend to their care and attentive consideration, entreating them to bear in mind the peculiar mercy of Providence in preserving them from all affright and terror during the series of wonderful disturbances that surrounded them, wishing them to be assured the veracity of their mother was pure and

undoubted, that even in her infancy it was in the family a proverb, and according to the testimony of that excellent person Chancellor Hoadly she was truth itself; she writes, not to gratify vanity, but to add weight to her relation.

To the Almighty and Unerring Judgment of Heaven and Earth I dare appeal for the truth, to the best of my memory and comprehension, of what I here relate.

Mary Ricketts.

MYSTERIOUS NOISES AND VISITORS

Soon after we were settled at Hinton I frequently heard noises in the night, as of people shutting, or rather slapping doors with vehemence. Mr. Ricketts went often round the house on supposition there were either housebreakers or irregularity among his servants. In these searches he never could trace any person; the servants were in their proper apartments, and no appearance of disorder. The noises continued to be heard, and I could conceive no other cause than that some of the villagers had false keys to let themselves in and out at pleasure; the only preventive to this evil was changing the locks, which was accordingly done, yet without the effect we had reasonably expected.

About six months after we came thither, Elizabeth Brelsford, nurse to our eldest son, Henry, then about eight months old, was sitting by him when asleep, in the room over the pantry, appropriated for the nursery, and, being a hot summer's evening, the door was open that faces the entrance into the yellow bedchamber, which, with the adjoining dressing-room, was the apartment usually occupied by the lady of the house. She was sitting directly opposite to this door, and plainly saw (as she afterwards related) a gentleman in a drab-coloured suit of clothes go into the yellow room. She was in no way surprised at the time, but on the housemaid, Molly Newman, coming up with her supper, she asked what strange gentleman was come. Upon the other answering there was no one, she related what is already described, and desired her fellow-servant to accompany her to search the room; this they did immediately without any appearance of what she had seen. She was much concerned and disturbed, and she was thoroughly assured she could no ways be deceived, the light being sufficient to distinguish any object clearly.

In some time after it was mentioned to me. I treated it as the effect of fear or superstition, to which the lower class of people are so prone, and it was entirely obliterated from my mind till the late astonishing disturbances brought to my recollection this and other previous circumstances. In the autumn of the same year George Turner, son of the gardener of that name, who was then groom, crossing the great hall to go to bed, saw at the other end a man in a drab-coloured coat, whom he concluded to be the butler, who wore such coloured clothes, he being lately come and his livery not made.

As he passed immediately upstairs to the room where all the men servants lay, he was in great astonishment to find the butler and the other men servants in bed. Thus the person he had seen in the hall remained unaccounted for, like the same person before described by the nurse; and George Turner, now living, avers these particulars in the same manner he first related them. In the month of July, 1767, about seven in the evening, there were sitting in the kitchen, Thomas Wheeler, postilion; Ann Hall, my own woman; Sarah, waiting woman to Mrs. Mary Poyntz; and Dame Lacy; the other servants were out, excepting the cook, then employed in washing up her things in the scullery.

A FEMALE
FIGURE

The persons in the kitchen heard a woman come downstairs, and along the passage leading towards them, whose clothes rustled as of the stiffest silk; and on their looking that way, the door standing open, a female figure rushed past, and out of the house door, as they conceived. Their view of her was imperfect; but they plainly distinguished a tall figure in dark-coloured clothes. Dame Brown, the cook, instantly coming in, this figure passed close by her, and instantly disappeared She described the person and drapery as before mentioned, and they all united in astonishment who or what this appearance could be; and their surprise was heightened

when a man, coming directly through the yard and into the house the way she went out, on being asked who the woman was he met, declared he had seen no one. Ann Hall, since married to John Sparks, now living at Rogate, near Petersfield, will testify to the truth of this relation, as will Dame Brown, now living at Bramdean. The postilion is since dead.

Meanwhile, the noises continued to be heard occasionally. Miss Parker's woman, Susan Maidstone, was terrified with the most dismal groans and rustling round her bed. At different times most of the servants were alarmed with noises that could no way be accounted for. In the latter end of the year 1769 Mr. Ricketts went to Jamaica; I continued at Hinton with my three infant children and eight servants...

PERSONAL
RESOLVE

...In the summer of 1770, on one night that I was lying in the yellow bedchamber (the same I have mentioned that the person in drab-coloured clothes was seen to enter) I had been in bed half an hour thoroughly awake, and without the least terror or apprehension on my spirits. I plainly heard the footsteps of a man with plodding step, walking towards the foot of my bed. I thought the danger too near to ring my bell of assistance, but sprang out of bed and in an instant was in the nursery opposite; and with Hannah Streeter (one of the servants) and a light I returned to search for what I had heard, but all in vain. There was a light burning in the dressing room within as usual and there was no door or means of escape save at the one that opened to the nursery. This alarm perplexed me more than any preceding, being within my own room, the footsteps as distinct as ever I heard, myself perfectly awake and collected.

I had nevertheless resolution to go to bed alone in the same room, and did not form any conclusion as to the cause of this very extraordinary disturbance. For some months afterwards I did not hear any noise that particularly struck my attention, till, in November of the same year, I think being removed to the chintz bedroom over the hall, as a warmer apartment, I once or twice heard sounds of harmony, and one night in particular I heard three distinct and violent knocks as given with a club, or something very ponderous, against a door below stairs; it occurred to me that a housebreaker must be forcing into some apartment, and I immediately rang my bell. No one hearing the summons, and the noise ceasing,

I thought no further of it at that time. After this, and in the beginning of the year 1771, I was frequently sensible of a hollow murmuring that seemed to possess the whole house; it was independent of wind, being equally heard on the calmest night, and it was a sound I had never been accustomed to hear.

TERRIFIED

On the morning of the 27th February, when Elizabeth Godin (another servant) came into my room, I inquired what weather. She replying in a very faint tone, I asked her if she was ill. She said she was well, but had never in her life been so terrified as during the preceding night that she had heard the most dismal groans and fluttering round her bed most part of the night, that she had got up to search the room and up the chimney and though it was bright moonlight she could not discover anything. I did not pay much attention to her account, but it occurred to me that should anyone tell her it was the room formerly occupied by Mrs. Parfait, the old housekeeper, she would be afraid to lie there again. Mrs. Parfait dying a few days before at Kilmston, was brought and interred at Hinton churchyard the evening of the night this disturbance happened.

That very day five weeks, being the 2nd of April, I waked between one and two o'clock, as I found by my watch, which, with a rushlight, was on a table close to my bedside, I lay thoroughly awake for some time, and then heard one or more persons walking to and fro in the lobby adjoining. I got out of bed and listened at the door for the space of twenty minutes, in which I distinctly heard the walking with the addition of a loud noise like a pushing against a door. Being thus assured my senses were not deceived, I determined to ring my bell, to which I had before much reluctance on account of disturbing the nursery maid, who was very ill of a fever.

UNEXPLAINED
PRESENCES

Elizabeth Godin during her illness lay in the room with my sons, and came immediately on hearing my bell. Thoroughly convinced there were persons in the lobby, before I opened my door, I asked her if she saw no one there. On her replying, in the negative, I went out to her, examined the window, which was shut, looked under the couch, the only furniture of concealment there; the chimney board was fastened, and when removed, all was clear behind it. She found the door into the lobby shut, as it was every night. After this examination I stood in

the room, pondering with much astonishment, when suddenly the door that opens into the little recess leading to the yellow apartment sounded as if played to and fro by a person standing behind it. This was more than I could bear unmoved. I ran into the nursery and rang the bell there that goes into the men's apartments. Robert Camis (a man servant) came to the door at the landing place, which door was every night secured, as that no person could get to that floor unless through the windows. Upon opening the door to Robert I told him the reason I had to suppose that some one was intrenched behind the door I before mentioned, and giving him a light and arming him with a billet of wood, myself and Elizabeth Godin waited the event. Upon opening the door there was not any being whatever, and the yellow apartment was locked, the key hanging up and a great bolt drawn across the outside door, as usual when not in use. There was then no further retreat or hiding place. After dismissing Robert and securing the door, I went to bed in my sons' room, and about half-an-hour afterwards heard three distinct knocks, as described before; they seemed below, but I could not then or ever after ascertain the place. The next night I lay in my own room; I now and then heard noises and frequently the hollow murmur.

On the 7th of May, exactly the day five weeks from the 2nd of April, this murmur was uncommonly loud. I could not sleep, apprehending it the prelude to some greater noise. I got up and went to the nursery, stayed there till half-an-hour past three, and then, being daybreak, I thought I should get some sleep in my own apartment; I returned and lay till ten minutes before four, and then

the great hall door directly under me was slapped to with the utmost violence, so as to shake my room perceivably. I jumped out of bed to the window that commands the porch, there was light to distinguish every object, but none to be seen that could account for what I had heard. Upon examining the door it was found fast locked and bolted as usual.

From this time I determined to have my woman lie in a little bed in my room. The noises grew more frequent, and she was always sensible of the same sounds, and much in the same direction as they struck me. Harassed and perplexed, I was yet very unwilling to divulge my embarrassment. I had taken every method to investigate the cause, and could not discover the least appearance of trick; on the contrary, I became convinced it was beyond the power of any mortal agent to perform, but, knowing how exploded such opinions were, I kept them in my own bosom, and hoped my resolution would enable me to support whatever might befall.

After midsummer the noises became every night more intolerable. They began before I went to bed and with intermissions were heard till after broad day in the morning. I could frequently distinguish articulate sounds, and usually a shrill female voice would begin, and then two others with deeper and manlike tone seemed to join in the discourse, yet though this conversation sounded as if close to me, I never could distinguish words.

STRANGE NOISES

I have often asked Elizabeth Godin if she heard any noise, and of what sort. She as often described the seeming conversation in the manner I have related, and other noises. One night in particular my bed curtains rustled, and sounded as if dragged by a person walking against them. I then asked her if she heard any noise and of what kind. She spoke of it exactly in the manner I have done. Several times I heard sounds of harmony in the room—no distinct or regular notes, but a vibration of harmonious tones; walking, talking, knocking, opening and slapping of doors were repeated every night. My brother (after-wards Earl of St. Vincent), who had not long before returned from the Mediterranean, had been to stay with me, yet so great was my reluctance to relate anything beyond the bounds of probability that I could not bring myself to disclose my embarrassed situation to the friend and brother who could most essentially serve and comfort me. The noises continuing in the same manner when he was with with me, I wished to learn

if he heard them, and one morning I carelessly said: "I was afraid last night the servants would disturb you, and rang my bell to order them to bed." He replied he had not heard them. The morning after he left me to return to Portsmouth, about three o'clock and daylight, Elizabeth Godin and myself both—she had been sitting up in bed looking round her, expecting as she always did to see something terrible—I heard with infinite astonishment the most loud, deep, tremendous noise, which seemed to rush and fall with infinite velocity and force on the lobby floor adjoining to my room. I started up, and called to Godin, "Good God! did you hear that noise?" She made no reply; on repeating the question, she answered with a faltering voice, "She was so frightened she scarce durst speak." Just at the instant we heard a shrill and dreadful shriek, seeming to proceed from under the spot where the rushing noise fell, and repeated three or four times, growing fainter as it seemed to descend, till it sank into earth. Hannah Streeter, who lay in the room with my children, heard the same noises, and was so appalled she lay for two hours almost deprived of sense and motion.

Having heard little of the noises preceding, and that little she did not regard, she had rashly expressed a wish to hear more of them, and from that night till she quitted the house there was scarce a night passed that she did not hear the sound as if some person walked towards her door, and pushed against it, as though attempting to force it open. This alarm, so more than commonly horrible, determined me to impart the whole series to my brother on his return to Hinton, expected in a week. The frequency of the noises, harassing to my rest, and getting up often at unreasonable hours, fixed a slow fever and deep cough, my health was much impaired, but my resolution firm. I remained in anxious expectation of my brother, and he being detained a week longer at Portsmouth than he had foreseen, it occurred to me to endeavour, by changing my apartment to obtain, a little rest; I removed to that formerly occupied by Elizabeth Godin; I did not mention my intention till ten at night, when the room was prepared, and I went to bed soon after. I had scarce lain down when the same noises surrounded me that I before have related, and I mention the circumstance of changing my room without previous notice, to prove the impossibility of a plan of operations being so suddenly conveyed to another part of the house were they such as human agents could achieve. The week following I was comforted by the arrival of my brother. However desirous to impart the narrative, I yet I forbore till the next morning; I wished him to enjoy a night's rest, and therefore contented myself with preparing him to hear on the morrow the most astonishing tale that ever assailed his ears, and that he must summon all his trust of my veracity to meet my relation. He replied it was scarce possible for me to relate any matter he could not believe, little divining the nature of what I had to offer to his faith.

CREEPY ENCOUNTERS

The next morning I began my narrative, to which he attended with mixed surprise and wonder. Just as I had finished, Captain Luttrell, our neighbour at Kilmston, chancing to call, induced my brother to impart the whole to him, who in a very friendly manner offered to unite his endeavours to investigate the cause. It was then agreed that he should come late in the evening, and I divide the night watch between them, keeping profoundly secret there was any such intention. My brother took the precaution, accompanied by his own servant, John Bolton, to go into every apartment, particularly those on the first attic storey, examined every place of concealment and saw each door fastened, save those to chambers occupied by the family; this done, he went to bed in the room over the servant's hall.

Captain Luttrell and my brother's man with arms sat up late in the chintz room adjoining, and my brother was to be called on any alarm.

I lay that night in Elizabeth Godin's room, and the children in the nurseries; thus every chamber on that floor was occupied. I bolted and locked the door that opened to that floor from the back stairs so that there was no entrance unless through the room where Captain Luttrell kept watch.

So soon as I lay down, I heard a rustling as of a person close to the door. I ordered Elizabeth Godin to sit up a while, and if the noise continued, to go and acquaint Mr. Luttrell.

She heard it, and instantly Mr. Luttrell's room door was thrown open, and we heard him speak. I must now give his account as related to my brother and myself the next morning.

He said he heard the footsteps of a person walking across the lobby, that he instantly threw the door open, and called. "Who goes there?" That something flitted past him when my brother directly called out, "Look against my door." He was awake, and heard what Mr. Luttrell had said, and also the continuance of the same noise till it reached his door. He arose and joined Mr. Luttrell.

Both astonished, they heard various other noises, examined everywhere, found the staircase door fast secured as I had left it. I lay so near, and had never closed my eyes, no one could go to that door unheard. My brother and his man proceeded upstairs, and found the servants in their own rooms, and all doors closed as they had seen just before. They sat up together, my brother and Mr. Luttrell till break of day, when my brother returned to his own chamber. About that time, as I imagined, I heard the chintz room door opened and slammed to with the utmost violence, and immediately that of the hall chamber opened and shut in the same manner. I mentioned to Godin my surprise that my brother, who was ever attentive not to alarm or disturb the children, should hazard both by such vehement noise. An hour after, l heard the house door open and slam in the same way, so as to shake the house. No one person was then up, for as I had never slept, I heard the servants rise and go down about half an hour afterwards.

BANGING DOORS

When we were assembled at breakfast, I observed the noise my brother had made with the doors.

Mr. Luttrell replied, "I assure you, Jervis made not the least noise; it was your door and the next I heard opened and slapped in the way you describe."

My brother did not hear either. He afterwards acknowledged to me that when gone to bed and Mr. Luttrell and I were sitting below, he heard dreadful groans and various noises that he was then and after unable to account for. His servant was at that time with mine below.

Captain Luttrell declared the disturbances of the preceding night were of such a nature that the house was an unfit residence for any human being. My brother, though more guarded in his expressions, concurred in that opinion, and the result of our deliberations was to send an express to Mr. Sainsbury, Lady Hillsborough's steward, to request he would come over immediately on a very particular occasion, with which he would be made acquainted on his arrival.

Unluckily, Dr. Sainsbury was confined with the gout and sent over his clerk, a youth of fifteen, to whom we judged it useless and improper to divulge the circumstances.
My brother sat up every night of the week he then passed at Hinton. In the middle of one of these nights, I was surprised with the sound of a gun or pistol let off near me, immediately followed by groans as of a person in agonies or expiring, that seemed to proceed between my chamber and the next, the nursery. I sent Godin to Nurse Horner, to ask if she had heard any noise; she had not. Upon my inquiry the next morning of my brother, he had not heard it, though the report and groans were loud and deep.

Several instances occurred where very loud noises were heard by one or two persons, when those equally near and in the same direction were not sensible of the least impression.

IMMENSE WEIGHT

As the watching every night made it necessary for my brother to gain rest in the day, he usually lay down after dinner. During one of these times he was gone to rest, I had sent the children and their attendants out to walk, the dairymaid gone to milk, the cook In the scullery, my own woman with my brother's man sitting together in the servants' hall; I, reading in the parlour heard my brother's bell ring with great quickness. I ran to his room, and he asked me if I had heard any noise, "because," said he, "as I was lying wide awake, an immense weight seemed to fall through the ceiling to the floor just by that mahogany press, and it is impossible I should be deceived." His man was by this time come up, and said he was sitting underneath the room as I before mentioned, and heard not the least noise. The inquiry and attention my brother devoted to investigate this affair was such as from the reach of his capacity and ardent spirit might he expected; the result was his earnest request that I would quit the place, and when he obliged me to return to Portsmouth, that I would permit him to send Mr. Nichols, his Lieutenant of Marines, and an old friend of the family, to continue, till my removal, with me.

One circumstance is of a nature so singularly striking that I cannot omit to relate it. In one of our evening's conversations on this wonderful train of disturbances, I mentioned a very extraordinary effect I had frequently observed in a favourite cat that was usually in the parlour with, me, and when sitting on table or chair with accustomed unconcern she would suddenly slink down as if struck with the greatest terror, conceal herself under my chair, and put her head close to my feet. In a short space of time she would come forth quite unconcerned. I had not long given him this account before it was verified to him in a striking manner. We neither then, nor I at other times, perceived the least noise that could give alarm to the animal, nor did I ever perceive the like effect before these disturbances, nor afterwards when she was removed with me to another habitation. The servants gave the same account of a spaniel that lived in the house, but to that, as I did not witness, I cannot testify.

[After this, Mrs. Ricketts left the house, which subsequently had only one tenant, a, Mr. Lawrence, who stayed about a year, and then suddenly quitted It.

After this the house was never occupied. On being pulled down there was found by the workmen under the floor of one of the rooms a small skull, said to be that of a monkey; but the matter was never brought forward by any regular inquiry, or professional opinion resorted to as to the real nature of the skull.]

IMPRESSIVE ACCOUNT

Thus the extraordinarily detailed and well witnessed report of the haunting of Hinton Ampner Manor House came to its conclusion.

What I find really impressive about this account is the detail, and the way the writer set about so diligently compiling statements and letters from servants and friends in order to record the haunting properly.

The question to ask is, was the report true or was it an extremely well produced hoax? Was it an epistolary style of tale designed to scare people as the Christmas season drew in?

If so, it is extremely well done, with very realistic multiple sources. It certainly wasn't treated as fiction, and was referred to in the regional and national press at the time as a genuine story.

Which leaves the question whether this was an "in joke" perpetrated by the publishers?

It is possible, but it is a dangerous thing to show bad faith to your readership by deliberately playing a trick on them, thus risking future credibility. It is unlikely that the *Gentleman's Magazine* would have gone out of its way to deceive. Indeed, when the letters came to light, they appear to have been treated with the utmost respect by the publishers.

In the context of the rise of Spiritualism at this time, it may well have been that the editors decided it was the right time to publish. By the same token, it would not have been the right time to publish a hoax.

What I will say is if the events reported are true, then the fact that the old manor house at Hinton Ampner is now gone is something I have mixed feelings about.

On the one hand, how interesting it would have been to find out more about those strange phenomena.

On the other hand, what a relief it has gone!

So: a true account? Or an elaborate piece of fiction written as the snows of winter begin to move in?

Once more, you decide!

16
A BRIEF THANK YOU AND GOODBYE

THE TRUTH..?

Whilst some stories in this book are explicable, many appear not to be.

The tantalising possibility that there's something more to our world than what we see in the cold light of day has been a fascination for people throughout the centuries. Indeed, many before us may well have considered some of the very same mysteries we've looked at in these pages.

We are travellers, then, on a well-trodden path that perhaps casts a light as much on human nature and our need for the mysterious, unusual and strange as on the world "out there", where the truth may or may not lie!

Whatever the causes of the sightings and phenomena reported in this book, be they the results of simple misunderstandings, a desire to hoodwink, the need to write a good story on a slow news day, Chinese whispers leading to unintended distortions - or genuine unexplained phenomena, these stories give us the chance to consider the nature of truth, how everybody shapes the world with the stories they tell, and how easy it is to smuggle fake news in alongside honest fact.

That's something we probably all need to remember in the modern day, with its conspiracy theories and accusations and distortions of truth!

MORE MYSTERIES!

Although this book has come to a close, it doesn't mean the end of our journey into the Mysteries of Portsmouth.

Maybe you have stories you'd like to tell, or you've seen strange and unusual phenomena you'd like to share with others? If so, join the Mysteries of Portsmouth facebook group and share what you've seen and heard.

Folk tales, urban legends, UFOs, ghosts, hauntings, poltergeists, myths, archaeology, crypto-zoology, witchcraft - whatever you've experienced, I'm sure there are many who'd love to read and hear about it.

You'll find the Mysteries of Portsmouth facebook group here:

www.facebook.com/groups/MysteriesOfPortsmouth/

I hope you've enjoyed this survey through history of the strange, the bizarre, the unusual and the mysterious. Maybe we'll meet again in other books I've written about Pompey!

I know for sure through my research of such phenomena there are plenty more ghost stories and strange tales related to Portsmouth, Hampshire and beyond, waiting to be enjoyed. Perhaps, one day, they will be the subject for future books!

Until then - goodbye, and thank you for your company!

Matt Wingett, October 2019

more books and talks from
www.lifeisamazing.co.uk

These books are available from my website, and I am happy to give iillustrated talks on any of these subjects. I also offer guided tours of Portsmouth.

Contact Matt Wingett through Life Is Amazing for details

Portsmouth, A Literary and Pictorial Tour
Matt Wingett

Join Matt Wingett on a tour through the streets and literature of Portsmouth.

Discover what Dickens, Kipling, Wells, Conan Doyle, Shute, Wodehouse, Beatrix Potter, Jane Austen, Mahatma Gandhi and many more writers had to say about Pompey, in this friendly and informal guide to the literature and writers of Portsmouth.

Paperback, £12.50
ISBN 978-0-9956394-8-5

Recollections of John Pounds
Henry Hawkes

John Pounds's influence was felt worldwide through his work as an educator, with his example eventually leading to the founding of Universal State Education in Britain.

This is the only firsthand account of the life of the educator who changed the school system in the UK by teaching poor children to read and write in his cobbler's shop in Old Portsmouth. An extraordinary account of life in Portsmouth in the 1830s.

Paperback, £9.99
ISBN 978-0-9572413-9-8

Conan Doyle and the Mysterious World of Light
Matt Wingett

In 1887, the very same year his first Sherlock Holmes novel, A Study In Scarlet was published, Sir Arthur Conan Doyle converted to Spiritualism while living in Southsea.

Discover why Conan Doyle converted, and the extraordinary effect it would have on the rest of his life.

Paperback, £12.99 ISBN 978-0-9572413-5-0
Hardback, £25 ISBN 978-0-9572413-8-1
Deluxe Limited Edition, £50

The History of Portsmouth
Lake Allen

The first really decent history of Portsmouth, from the pen of Lake Allen, close friend to Sir Frederick Madden, and a Portsmouth obsessive.

Written in 1817, The History of Portsmouth traces the earliest appearances of the area in history in 501 AD, through the Middle Ages to 1814.

An amazing achievement.

Paperback, £9.99
ISBN 978-0-9572413-6-7

Ten Years In A Portsmouth Slum
Robert Dolling

The Rev Robert Dolling was sent to Portsmouth in 1885 on missionary work in Landport. Discover the the extraordinary lives he encountered and follow the story of the community he worked with in one of the "worst towns of the British Empire". An uplifting true account of the man who touched so many lives in Landport.

Paperback, 9.99
ISBN 978-0-9572413-4-3

A Study In Scarlet
Beeton's Christmas Annual 1887
Facsimile Edition
Arthur Conan Doyle

There are only 11 complete copies of the first edition of the very first Sherlock Holmes novel.

This volume is a faithful facsimile, including colour adverts and the other stories and plays published with the original.

Great for the Holmes collector!

Paperback, £15.00
ISBN 978-1-913001-00-1

more books and talks from
www.lifeisamazing.co.uk

The Snow Witch
A Portsmouth Novel
Matt Wingett

A young woman on the run arrives in Portsmouth in a freak snow storm. A refugee from a deeply traumatic past, in the course of protecting herself in a snowbound Portsmouth, we discover she is a far more powerful woman than even she realised. This book has inspired an art show and live events and is highly recommended. Contains sexual violence. Not for children.

Paperback, £9.99 ISBN 978-0-9956394-5-4
Hardback, £19.99 ISBN 978-0-9956394-6-1

By Celia's Arbour
A Tale of Portsmouth Town
Walter Besant and James Rice

This novel, first published in 1877, is a story of love, loss, intrigue, spies and revolution, set in the naval town of Portsmouth.
Walter Besant was born in the town, and the detailed scenes of life in Portsmouth before the town walls were demolished is pitched beautifully. A fascinating story, full of lyrical writing.

Paperback, £14.99
ISBN 978-0-9572413-7-4

Portsmouth Fairy Tales for Grown Ups
Edited by Tessa Ditner

A collection of short stories based in the city of Portsmouth, ranging from the hilarious to the bizarre - but all responding to the idea of the Fairy Tale.
From vengeful dolls, through to Victorian detectives and science fiction dystopias, this book never fails to surprise and delight.
A map on the back shows the locations of the different stories.

Paperback, £9.99
ISBN: 978-0-9572413-3-6

Dark City
Portsmouth Tales of Haunting and Horrow
Edited by Karl Bell and Stephen Pryde-Jarman

This collection of horror stories is set in Portsmouth, and varies from the spine-chilling through the unsettling to the strange.

A gripping visit to the strange and bizarre side of the city of Portsmouth.

Paperback, £9.99
ISBN 978-0-9956394-0-9

Day of the Dead
Tales of Death and Dying to Disturb, Perturb and Delight
Portsmouth Writers' Hub

Every year, Portsmouth Writers' Hub tells ghostly and strange stories in Portsmouth's Square Tower.
This collection of tales looks at the strange and macabre side of life, sometimes with grim humour.
Powerful writing from some of the extraordinary talent to be found in Portsmouth,

Paperback, £9.99
ISBN 978-0-9956394-1-6

A Pompey Person's Guide to
Everything Great About Southampton

A novelty book that promises to tell you all the finer things about Southampton as seen through the eyes of a Portsmouth person. Of course, when you look inside, the little book is blank!

Paperback, £5.00

ISBN 978-0-9956394-2-3

EXCITING UPCOMING PUBLICATIONS

I have a passion for Portsmouth history and have republished some of the more scarce Portsmouth-related works. I also write fiction and have produced several books set in Portsmouth. All are published through Life Is Amazing and are available from **wwwlifeisamazing.co.uk** post-free in the UK.

The list below is of titles not yet published at time of writing, but intended for release.

FICTION:

Charlotte Temple, Susannah Haswell Rowson
A Metrical History of Portsmouth, Henry Slight
The Great Salterns, Sarah Doudney

NON-FICTION:

From Prison Dock to Portsmouth Dockyard, Anon
Portchester Castle, Its Origin, History and Antiquities, Anon
The Autobiography of Sir Walter Besant, Sir Walter Besant
The Narrative of the Loss of the Royal George at Spithead, 1782, Anon

PRINTS FROM LIFE IS AMAZING

Reprints of classic Portsmouth scenes are also available from our shop. If you would like copies please go:

www.lifeisamazing.co.uk

We offer a selection of different sizes, with many images available as large prints.

A NOTE ON THE ILLUSTRATIONS IN THIS BOOK

The illustrations from this book are from my personal collection, or are drawn from the public domain via Wikimedia Commons, with the following exceptions:
p.18, p.19, UFO images, courtesy pixabay.com
p.24, Tutankhamun, courtesy Roland Unger

Acknowledgments

I would like to thank the story-tellers, historians, journalists and everyone who, over the years, wrote down a more or less accurate draft of history from which I could mine gems for this book.

On a less abstract level, I'd like to thank my dad, who is an honest beta-reader and tells me when things aren't right. Also, thanks to Amelia Clarke for providing me with a drawing for the UFO on the cover of this book, and to all my friends on facebook who gave honest opinions when I was trying out new cover designs. You know who you are.

Thanks, too, to everyone who expressed an interest in this book when I first mentioned it, and who told me they'd buy a copy if ever I published it.

I will hold you to that. ;)

Finally, thank you to Jackie, who once again came home from work over an intensive four week period to find piles of musty old books on the dining room table that were waiting for me to scan them for artwork. I thank you, Jackie, for being willing to put up with eating while squeezed between tottering towers of books, and coming home from time away to find yet more books in bed where I'd dozed off reading them.

Actually, Jackie, you are a gem, and this octopus is for you and you alone. xxx:

Lightning Source UK Ltd.
Milton Keynes UK
UKHW050821010422
400924UK00002B/36